ASSISTED DYING

Chuck & Judy   Ps. 71:9
We seem to have gotten old
before our time, but we
can still love each other·
as friends & believers.

K. MERTON CLAAR

Ken

Xulon
PRESS

PROLOGUE

T he hardest things for Arlen to get adjusted to were the nights at Meadowview. He had thought it would be pretty quiet on the third floor, but instead there were all sorts of peculiar noises. After a month, the one that bugged him the most was some type of persistent soft hum that was in his ears all night long. He had decided it must be some kind of air conditioner.

But tonight he heard another sound. Someone was crying. He sat up in bed and turned his head back and forth, trying to localize the sounds. He was pretty sure they came from Mrs. Toskini next door, but he couldn't be positive because sound can travel a long way at night. He doubted it was the man on the other side, even though they had never met. He finally decided he couldn't do anything about it, so he lay back down and tried to get in a comfortable position to sleep.

He woke up stiff and sore, and it took him awhile to get up and organized. Then he thought, *I ought to go and see what's wrong next door. It doesn't seem right for her to have to cry alone.* He wasn't sure what he was going to say, but no use waiting for inspiration. He would just stick his ex-reporter's nose in and see what he could see.

He shuffled his walker to the door that was next closest to his and rapped lightly. The door swung open a little. He was embarrassed, because suddenly he had a 'senior moment' and couldn't remember her name. So he called out "Ma'am are you in there?" No answer. He shoved the door open a little further with his walker. He felt a little guilty, but rationalized again that it was just his old reporter's nose acting up, and that she might really need help.

Her room was just the reverse of his and otherwise identical, except for the furnishings and the pictures. She had obviously been there a while. There was a tall antique oak dresser on the wall next to the bathroom door. It was covered with so many framed photographs that there wasn't a square inch of the top showing. Behind that was a hospital bed, the type that adjusts six ways from Sunday. Her bookcases were also antique oak and stuffed full of books of all sizes. More photos stuck in wooden frames lined the top of them and on the wall behind those frames a bright collage of photos covered a tan corkboard. *This lady knew a lot of people*, he thought. As he pushed further into the room, the first thing he noticed was her wheelchair lying on its side in the far corner of the room. Then he spotted her. She was lying almost beside the bed. Her neck was bent way over her right shoulder and her body lay twisted almost double. She was wearing a faded blue flannel nightgown that was pushed up around her hips and no robe or cover. He thought, *she looks so tiny and frail. It looks like her neck is broken.* He shuffled over to her as fast as his walker allowed and slowly bent down and grabbed her pale bluish hand that was lying limp across her stomach. He couldn't find a pulse so he struggled to put his ear up to her mouth, but when he couldn't feel any breath stir at all he quickly decided that he shouldn't touch anything else.

He struggled back to his feet and pushed his walker over to the big red emergency button sticking out of the wall by the bed. He punched it hard several times and then had to sprawl out on the bed because his legs were beginning to refuse to hold him up. Even his walker wasn't enough at those times.

CHAPTER 1

Only the previous month Arlen had entered the of Meadowview Assisted Living Center prepared to hate the place and everything associated with it, but the young woman who greeted him so pleasantly at the front desk softened his mind just a little.

"Good Morning. You must be Mr. Arlen. I'm Mia. Welcome to Meadowview."

"Thanks, Mia. This is my nephew George. He's helping me get moved in." Arlen waved toward the tall young man who was standing beside him holding a small suitcase.

Mia grabbed a key from a box on the desk and said, "Come along, I'll show you to your suite. It's on the third floor. The elevators are down this way." She walked around the desk and started off down the middle hallway. Arlen grasped his walker and shuffled after her with George bringing up the rear.

As the elevator door opened on the third floor Arlen was impressed with the peaceful landscape paintings that hung along the hallway. They moved about halfway down and came to a door on the left that had a hand painted sign on it that said 'Jason Arlen'. Mia unlocked the door and pushed it open. The room wasn't large, but as he shuffled in, he was pleasantly surprised at how bright and airy it was. He smiled a little because he knew he had been expecting institutional green with posters on the wall. Instead, a beautiful seascape scene that matched those in the hall greeted his eyes as he shuffled into the room. The seascape colors blended perfectly with the blues and greens of the carpet. "We have already put your bags in the closet, Mr. Arlen. If you need help getting them put away just give us a call. We always have someone willing to help." Jason huffed, "I can still take care of myself. I don't need any help." He thought to himself, *as long as George is here.*

Mia smiled at him and said, "That's wonderful that you are able to do things for yourself, but please let us help you when you need it." She turned and left the room.

George put the small bag down on the bed. He had sent Arlen's sparse furniture ahead so it would be there when they arrived. "Well, Uncle Arlen, what do you think?"

"What do you expect me to think? It's a well-kept prison, but I'll get used to it, I guess. You could have done worse."

"Hardly a prison. It looks pretty nice to me."

"That's because you don't have to live here. I do." He shuffled over to the bed and pushed the small bag aside and plunked down on the spread, falling over on his side on the pillow.

"You okay, Unc?"

"Yeah. That's why I'm in here. My muscles don't work so well sometimes. I'm getting used to it. You don't have to stick around. Thanks for the help in getting me here. And thanks for all your great help in getting rid of my stuff that I can't use any more. I won't forget it."

"Hey, I was glad to help. I would still be glad to help, but you know that Beth and I will be moving back to Minnesota next week. So I want to get you all set up before we leave."

"You've done all you need to do. More than enough. These folks will take care of me like the senile old man they think I am. So I'll be okay. Go home and kiss Beth for me, and tell her thanks for putting up with me these last few weeks. It must have been very hard on her and the kids."

George walked over and slid the closet door open and pulled out a suitcase. "I'll help you unpack before I go. I can at least do that."

"You don't need to do that. I've got the rest of my life to unpack my suitcase. Go home."

"Don't get grumpy on me. I just want to help. Can't I unpack these suitcases?"

"I'm sorry. Why don't you just set them up on the bed with the little one, and I can take it from there. Come back and see me before you go. Bring Beth, if she will come. I'd like to thank her in person for all the help she has given me getting ready for this adventure."

George grabbed the two suitcases and lined them up on the bed. Then he turned and stuck out his hand, "I know you aren't happy with this move, Uncle Arlen, but I hope it works out really well for you. Beth and I will keep in touch and maybe next summer we can come back out for a short vacation. My job is going to be pretty intense for a while. I have to get used to new people and new ways of doing things. That will take some time." He shook Arlen's hand, put his hand over his eyes and whispered, "I'll miss you, Unc. We had lots of good times together."

Arlen forced a small smile and said, "come on, don't get mushy or you will break me up. I will miss you like the dickens. Now, get out of here." He pushed George toward the door.

After George had gone Arlen looked at the three suitcases sitting on the bed and thought, *that was a stupid thing to tell him to do. Now I can't lie down and I really need to.* He pulled his walker over and stood up. Turning back to the bed, he grabbed the handle of one of the big suitcases and pulled. The weight held it to the bed for a minute, and then it slid over and thumped onto the floor, dragging him down alongside of it. He lay there for a minute catching his breath and then pulled his walker over and stood up. *How in the world*

9

am I going to get that other big suitcase off the bed without killing myself? Oh well, here goes nothing. He grasped the handle of the other bag and tugged on it. But it was heavier and he couldn't move it. Finally he had to sit back down on the side of the bed. *What do I do now? I'm stuck.*

He sat for a minute beside the recalcitrant bag and rested his arm on it. He was startled by a quiet tap tap on his door. "Come on it, It isn't locked."

The door swung open and a very large black man stepped in and closed the door. "Hi, Mr. Arlen. Mia sent me up to see if I could help you in any way. She saw that your nephew had left, and those bags *are* kind of heavy."

Arlen laughed. "If I believed in angels I would say you are one. I just about wrecked myself getting this one bag on the floor, and I can't move the other one. Could you put it on the floor or somewhere for me so I can unload it? I really need to lie down now. By the way, please just call me Arlen if you would. What's your name?"

The big man strode over and grabbed the heavy bag and picked it up like it was empty and looked around. "Look here, Arlen, we have some suitcase stands down in the basement. I'll put this on the floor for now and be right back up with a couple of them. You lie down and take a rest. This moving in stuff is hard on the nerves. Oh yeah, I'm Ben. I'm not an angel, I'm one of the physical therapists here. When you get settled in, the gym is right down the hall on this floor."

"Thanks, Ben. I'm going to lie down now. Please just walk right back in when you get those stands. I'll appreciate not having to pick my clothes off the floor." He pushed the small bag onto the floor and stretched out on the bed. Before Ben came back with the stands he was sound asleep.

He didn't sleep as soundly the night he heard the sobbing.

CHAPTER 2

After only a couple of minutes Mia popped in the open doorway, cast a puzzled look at him lying on the bed and said, "Mr. Arlen, what's going on?"

He pointed to the pile that had been his neighbor and she rushed over and dropped to her knees beside her and gently touched the woman's neck.

"She's dead, Mr. Arlen, what happened?" She jerked a blanket off the foot of the bed and carefully spread it over Mrs. Toskini.

"I heard her crying really hard in the middle of the night, and so I came over this morning to see what was wrong, and if I could help her. Obviously I couldn't. I think her neck is broken."

Mia looked at him and said, "She must have fallen off the bed on her head and broke her neck."

"I don't think so. Look at the funny way she is lying. I think somebody broke her neck." He sat up and stared down at the blanket that covered the body.

"Why would anyone want to break an innocent woman's neck?" Mia said, standing up and walking over to face him.

"Well, for a start, have you seen some of those losers who hang around her room? I'd be afraid to be alone with a few of them, especially that guy with the ponytail and the big ugly tattoos."

Mia shrugged and turned and picked up the phone from the bedside table. She punched the big 911 button that was in the center of all of the Meadowview phones. As she calmly described the situation to the dispatcher, he noticed she didn't say a word about murder.

He found that the local police were pretty fast. It seemed like only a couple of minutes and the room was full of them. The first to arrive were two blue suits, then a big heavy-set sergeant, and finally a short, stocky lieutenant, who said his name was Crowder. The hair on both sides of his balding head was frizzed up and gray and he was sporting an old tan jacket with a gold badge on the lapel. He reminded Arlen of Colombo on that old TV show.

"Mr. Er—Arlen, how did you happen to discover the body?" His dark eyes drilled into Arlen's.

"I heard her crying last night, so this morning I came over to see why," he said, staring straight back.

"Are you a personal friend of this lady?"

"No, I have only eaten with her a few times, but I am her next door neighbor."

"How did you get into the room?" The cool question caused Arlen to glare at the lieutenant. "The door was ajar so I pushed it open and, when she didn't answer, I came in."

After a few minutes Arlen decided he had probably convinced the Lieutenant that he wasn't capable of pushing her out of her bed, but unfortunately, he could see that the lieutenant tended to believe Mia's theory that she had fallen out of bed and broken her neck.

The police doctor strode in a few minutes later in his starched white jacket and carrying the perquisite black bag. He looked her over and announced "her neck is broken. That is the probable cause of death." Then he picked his bag off the floor and strode out of the room.

"But Lieutenant, look how crooked her body is lying. She didn't just fall out of bed. And why is her wheelchair tipped over?"

"Well, maybe her death wasn't instantaneous, and she wiggled around a bit." He thought out loud as he picked up the blanket and took another quick glance at her before the morgue boys picked her up and slipped her into an anonymous black body bag and lay it on their roll-around gurney. Even after reporting on many deaths over the years, the sight of the lumpy body bag containing what was left of a once-upon-a-time nice old lady caused something deep in his brain to go black with depression. The lumps holding the bag up seemed to tell him that this whole life journey was pretty useless and that sooner or later he would be just another pile of body parts in another big black bag.

The lieutenant interrupted his reverie, saying, "Her tipped over wheelchair may not have anything to do with her death. She may had dumped it over when she got out of it to go to bed."

"Keep an open mind, Lieutenant, I think she was murdered."

"We always do Mr. Arlen, but this one doesn't look too difficult. The poor lady fell out of bed and broke her neck and then struggled a bit before she died." He closed his notebook and shoved it in his coat pocket and strode out the door.

As Arlen shuffled back to his room, Mia walked alongside of him. Finally, just as he pulled open his door she said, "You still don't believe she fell out of bed, do you?"

"No. I don't see how she could have ended up in that position by just falling out of bed. Besides, if she fell and broke her neck, she wouldn't have been able to move around into the position we found her in. There is also her tipped over wheelchair to consider."

"Well, try and forget about it. She probably just twisted as she fell and that's how she ended up. But we likely will never know exactly how it happened." She smiled and waved and headed toward the elevators.

As Arlen closed his door he thought about how calmly Mia had taken Mrs. Toskini's death, and he wondered how many other deaths she had handled as the manager of Meadowview.

Shuffling toward his bed, he tripped over a small fold in the rug and had to scramble to keep from falling on the floor. He thought, *I guess I'm getting used to that now, but it still pumps the old adrenaline flow because I know that sooner or later I will fall like the lady in the old TV commercial and not be able to get up.*

He took a couple of Ibuprofen for the extra pain and lay back on his narrow bed. As he lay there he took another survey of his small empire. He did that often because he got bored easily and yet his energy level didn't match his mind's desire to get up and do things.

His old roll-top desk bulged out from the wall that enclosed the bathroom. It was the only piece of real furniture he had brought with him from his old house. It was the kind you could see in antique stores, beautiful golden oak with a scarred top that was at least an inch thick. He chuckled as he remembered the trouble they had when they brought it in. They had to take it apart and rebuild it in the room. It was majestic sitting there. Of course, it was way too big for the room, but he just had to have one memory of his productive days. He had spent many nights writing at that big desk. His phone was on the desktop too. A little inconvenient from his bed, but right now he couldn't afford a cell phone. George had told him that one day he would get him one and would bring him a laptop computer to replace his large PC, which he didn't bring with him. He was surprised that he missed writing and was looking forward to starting again. Then he thought, *I guess George won't bring me any of that stuff now that he is on his way to the other side of the world. Oh well.*

CHAPTER 3

A rlen's mind popped back to his neighbor and a surge of anger chugged its way up into the front of his mind. He thought, *how can I prove that nice lady was murdered? I can't get around like I used to and most of my investigative resources are gone, but I've just got to do something!* He needed to find himself some legs. He pulled himself up on the bed and grabbed his walker, thinking that the British had been right in calling it a 'Zimmer' frame. It was an odd name of an odd contraption, but it helped him move.

He stood up and thought, *I have to get into her room one more time and look around.* He knew Mia wouldn't let him in someone else's room, so he just shuffled out of his room and pushed his walker the short distance to his neighbor's door. He was surprised to find it ajar. He didn't hesitate to push the door open with his walker and start to shuffle on in. He stopped suddenly as a figure turned and looked up from the dresser drawer he was searching through.

"Hi, can I help you?"

Arlen was shocked to see that the man speaking was the guy with all of the tattoos.

"What the heck are you doing?" He barked, moving on into the room.

"I'm looking for Grandma's address book so we can notify people of her death," he said with no sign of annoyance. He moved closer to Arlen until he was standing looking down at him. It was then that Arlen realized he was a very big man, and that he was in a pretty risky position. He looked like he could break him in two and he could certainly outrun him. "What are *you* doing in here?" The man smiled as he said it.

Arlen thought quickly, "I saw your grandmother's door ajar and wanted to see what was going on. I didn't think anyone was supposed to be in here." It sounded feeble so he backed a ways toward the door.

"Well, I'm supposed to be here. The lady at the desk gave me the key." He smiled again as if the whole thing was a big joke.

"My name is Arlen, what's yours?" He hadn't been a reporter for years for nothing.

"I'm Stan Toskini. I'm taking care of the arrangements for my grandmother's funeral. Did you know her well?"

"No, I didn't really know her at all, I just moved in a short time ago, but I do know on the night of her murder she was crying in the middle of the night."

"Hmmm! You really think there was foul play?" Toskini said, leaning closer to Arlen.

"You bet. I don't believe she could have gotten herself into the position she was in when I found her. Someone did a real number on her. He must have been there when I heard her crying. How do I know it wasn't you?" A quick thought rushed through his mind, *I always ask too many questions.*

The tattooed man smiled, "I can understand how you might think that, but I was really very fond of her, and besides, I'm afraid I am in the business of saving lives, not taking them. I'm also very much afraid you may be right about it being murder, though. Grandma was doing something she wouldn't tell us about, and I saw several times that it was really scaring her."

He saw Arlen glancing down at his tattoos and laughed again. "I don't blame you. I don't look much like a lifesaver, do I? But I assure you, in my occupation I find these tattoos are a real benefit. You see, I have a ministry to motorcycle riders and gang members. We ride around the state and set up in truck stops and rest areas and witness about Jesus to anyone who will listen. If I looked like you nobody would. Listen, that is."

Arlen was flabbergasted. He was more used to the liberal pastors he had met who wore polyester jackets and dull ties or very expensive Italian suits, not tattoos and hair bands. He was sure that the motorcycle gang members he had met wouldn't listen to Mr. Polyester, but they might just listen to one of their own. He couldn't help wondering, though, what this guy's pitch was. Who would do something like that without an angle?

"Did you get those tattoos just for the purpose of getting into the field?" Arlen leaned on his walker. He was just about at the limit of his endurance.

Stan laughed again and motioned toward a chair. Arlen gratefully sank into it. "Thanks. My legs are pretty weak, but I am interested in what you are saying."

"No, I got these quite honestly. When I got out of the Navy, I was pretty wild. I hung out with a biker gang and we had our own tattoo artist. He was pretty good, but I think he was into pop art or some such. He loved big designs and bright colors. Unfortunately he gave me blood poisoning with his needle, and I ended up in the hospital for a spell. While I was in there, a chaplain took me on for his special care and spent a lot of time with me, and by the time I got out, Jesus had straightened my path. After that I went to Bible College and then sort of fell into this ministry. There are a lot of supposed tough guys out there who are in worlds of pain and heartache. I have found that only Jesus can sort it all out."

Arlen winced at the Jesus part, but said, "I guess I more or less understand where you are coming from, but what are we going to do about your grandmother's death?" He knew he had found his legs, if he could only get past those superstitions..

"I don't know. I was hoping there was something around here that would help, but so far I haven't found anything." Stan pointed back to the open dresser drawer.

Just then the door swung open and Mia stepped into the room. "Hi, how's it going?"

"I'm still looking for Gramma's address book, but so far no luck. Mr. Arlen here is helping me."

She gave Arlen a strange unreadable look and said, "Hello, Mr. Arlen, I hope you have decided your theory was mistaken. Mr. Arlen doesn't believe your grandmother died a natural death," she explained to Toskini.

"I understand that is so."

Arlen wondered why he didn't tell her he didn't believe it either, but he held his peace.

"Please bring the key back to the desk when you are through, Mr. Toskini. I will be at the desk for another hour. If you aren't finished by then we would prefer that you come back tomorrow." She gave him a big smile, spun around and walked out the door, closing it gently.

"Why didn't you tell her you didn't believe the natural death theory either?" Arlen asked him.

"I've learned that it is sometimes tough to tell who your friends are. I guess I tend to keep my speculations to myself until I am sure. We don't have any idea what happened yet or who is involved, so I'd just like to keep my options open. The Bible says 'he who holds his tongue is wise'."

"You're a lot smarter than I am, that's for sure. I tend to blab everything out, and I get in a whole lot of trouble sometimes." Arlen smiled and thought, *he must wonder about me*

*too, but probably has decided, like the lieutenant, that I'm
not much of a threat.*

"My Grandma had an address book that had hundreds of
names and numbers in it. I'm sure, if we can find it, we will
at least have a starting place. But so far I haven't been able
to come up with it, and there aren't many more places to look
in this little room."

"Have you looked in the bathroom?"

"No, I hadn't gotten that far yet. Could you go ahead and
look in there? I'll take another look in her desk, and then I
guess Mia wants us out of here. I'm a little curious as to why
she is so insistent that we leave, but I imagine it is in the rules
somewhere." He turned and pulled out the small chair and
sat down at the desk, grabbing a handful of papers out of the
middle cubbyhole.

Arlen shuffled over to the bathroom door and pushed it
wide open and switched on the light. The room was almost
exactly like his, except that it had one of those things on the
toilet seat to make it higher and easier to sit on. That was
something he thought he could use. He made a mental note
to ask Toskini what he was going to do with all of that kind
of stuff, but figured right then wasn't too sensitive a time to
do it. He noticed another difference from his place. This one
had a shower/tub combination, and the tub had a portable
seat with handrails across it so a person could sit and take a
shower. He looked around, but didn't see anything unusual.
The medicine cabinet was the only enclosed space, and it was
too small to hold anything much, so he turned to leave. As
he swung around, he tripped and barely caught hold of the
chrome handle of the bathtub seat. It moved a little, but held
his weight.

As he straightened up he could see a square black corner
sticking out from under the seat edge. He slowly bent over
and pulled it out into the light. It was a worn, well-used
address book.

He fantasized for a minute about hiding it from Toskini, but then decided he couldn't do much alone. He still needed his legs, so he hollered, "Hey, I found it! It was hidden in here."

Toskini came running into the bathroom, almost bowling Arlen over. "That's great! Let's see it."

Arlen reluctantly handed over the book, half expecting the man to run off with it. Instead he opened it and riffled through the pages.

"I don't see anything very unusual here, just a bunch of addresses, but there must have been some reason why she hid it." He held the book up and frowned at it.

"Yes, and she must have done it very shortly before she died. It isn't wet and it would have been right in the water dripping from the seat. I bet she put it there just before I heard her cry."

Toskini said, "Let's take it out of here and have a better look at it. There must be something in it she didn't want someone to see." He walked over and sat down at the desk.

Arlen followed him out and said, "I've got an idea, if you agree. It is pretty hard for us both to look at it at the same time. Why don't you leave it with me overnight, and I can take a good look at it. You can come back tomorrow, and I'll tell you if I've found anything. Then you can take a closer look at it and see if I've missed something. You know I'm not going anywhere."

Arlen could see that Toskini was mulling the idea over, but after a minute he said, "Well, I guess we have to trust each other a little, and I don't imagine you will run off with it. I have a meeting that will take up most of my evening, so go ahead and take it back to your room and study it, and I will take home the rest of these papers from the desk. Save me a place at the table for lunch tomorrow, and we can compare notes then." Toskini stood up and stuck out his hand. Arlen grabbed it and shook it and both men headed out the door. He managed to get back to his bed without tripping himself up, and, as he lay down with the book in his hand, he thought about that hospital bed next door. He would have to ask Toskini what he was going to do with it.

Boy, he marveled, *that old lady sure had a raft of family and friends*. There must have been two hundred names in her book. They looked very much like ordinary addresses, except that at least one on most pages had a symbol beside the last name. It was something like a blue crescent moon with a red handle on it. They were all hand colored, so it must have been a lot of work for her. Maybe she belonged to some kind of organization and that was their symbol. He really couldn't believe that Mrs. Toskini could have been involved in anything shady, at least shady enough to cause her death. It could be that they were just members of a bridge club. And yet, someone had killed her, and she had obviously hidden the book for a reason.

He dropped it on the bedside table and immediately fell into an exhausted sleep. He often fell asleep in his clothes because it was sometimes such a struggle to get them off.

He didn't know what time it was, but his brain registered a slight whisper of sound in the room. He was a pretty off-and-on sleeper, but because of the tiring day he had been through, it took him a few moments to wake up, and by that time there were no more noises. He tapped on the bedside lamp and looked around, but everything seemed okay, so he turned the light off and was soon sound asleep again.

CHAPTER 4

B y the time he woke up in the morning Arlen had forgotten about the book. He made his way to the bathroom and on his way back he remembered the adventure of the night before. He glanced down at the table, but couldn't see the book. He searched frantically all around his bed, but it was nowhere to be found. Then he remembered the swish in the middle of the night and he knew someone had come in and taken the book. At first he panicked, wondering what he was going to tell Toskini. Then his panic turned to fright as he realized that only Toskini and he had known about the book. And he was coming back today, maybe to finish him off. So much for his good guy line. *It was really hard,* he thought, *to associate the guy he had met yesterday with someone who would kill a little old lady, let alone his grandmother. But who else could have known that he had the book?* He was still chasing it around in his mind when he heard a loud knock on his door and hollered, "come in, it's not locked."

Toskini threw open the door and strode in, talking even before Arlen had a chance to sit up. "Something really strange is going on here, Mr. Arlen. While I was out at my meeting someone came in and trashed my place. They took the papers I had taken from grandma's desk, but there didn't seem to be anything in them anyway." He plunked down in Arlen's desk chair.

Arlen wasn't smiling as he said, "In a way, I'm glad to hear you say that, because it makes it easier for me to tell you what I have to say. Someone was in here last night and took the book. I heard him in the middle of the night but I didn't add it all up until I saw that the book was missing this morning."

Toskini jumped up and said, "That's very strange because only you and I know that you found that book. Who else could possibly have known? We didn't tell Mia or anyone else. Besides, what is so important about an address book?"

"I don't know, but it is pretty spooky. I don't like to think that people can pop in and out of my room whenever they feel like it."

Toskini moved over to the door. "I stopped and picked up grandma's key from Mia. Let's go and see if they did anything to her room. He headed out the door and Arlen got up, grabbed his walker and followed him.

Toskini started to shove the key into the lock and then stopped and held up his hand and whispered, "Hang on a minute, it isn't locked. Let me go in first."

Arlen didn't argue with that proposition. Toskini's muscular body and arms were convincing enough. Toskini shoved the door open and hurried in, and Arlen followed a little ways behind him. It didn't take long to see that no one was in the room, but that someone had been. The contents of the dresser and desk were strewn over the bed and all scrambled up. None of the photos had been disturbed, but Arlen had noticed before that there had been a vase of artificial geraniums on her bedside table. Now those flowers had been pulled out of the vase and thrown on the table. On the sidewall above her large dresser a picture had been removed. He looked around and found the picture leaning against the foot of the bed. He pulled it out and stared at the back of it. In the middle there was a small piece of magic tape that had been half pulled off.

He turned the picture and saw another piece dangling at the edge of the frame.

At the same time Toskini started yelling from the bathroom. Arlen hobbled in, and Stan pointed to the light fixture over the medicine cabinet. The light cover had been removed and laid down on the sink counter.

"What do you suppose all this is in aid of," Toskini asked, pointing at the light.

"I'm not sure, but I do remember once, when I was in a house that had been bugged, they hid the sensors in places just like these. I think this place was bugged last night when we discovered the book. They must have removed the bugs when they searched the room. They knew where the book was, but I imagine they trashed here, and in your place, to see if they could find anything else incriminating. Either that or we've got two groups interested in us."

"Yes, and it means we're not only dealing with a murderer, but with some sort of an organization. I wonder what in the world Grandma got herself involved in?"

"I don't know, but maybe I ought to call Lt. Crowder again. Perhaps he really does have an open mind." He got up and headed toward the door.

"I've got to go and meet some people, but here's my cell phone number, and if you can think of anything I can do give me a call. I can chase down most anything you think will help. Meanwhile, let's go down and get some of that good lunch that Meadowview is famous for."

After lunch, Arlen headed back to his room and settled down in his desk chair. He remembered that he had forgotten to ask Toskini about the hospital bed and other stuff. *Got to catch him before they move it all out*, he thought. He reached in the drawer and pulled out the phone book. He knew the police didn't like to be called on their 911 lines for administrative business, so he looked in the blue pages until he found their non-emergency number. When he finally got through, he was told that Crowder was out on a case. He knew that the officer had a cell phone, but he also knew he wasn't important enough to rate knowing that number. So he waited and waited until he was about to give up and go down to supper. Just as he reached the door, the phone rang. He had half a desire to ignore it and give him a taste of his own medicine, but he turned back, grabbed the phone off the desk, and said, "Arlen here."

"Hello, Mr. Arlen, what can I do for you?" The voice was civil, but certainly not warm.

"Hi, Lieutenant, I think I have some more information about the murder of Mrs. Toskini at Meadowview."

"You said murder again, Mr. Arlen. I still don't believe it, but tell me what you have to say and perhaps I might change my mind."

Arlen thought, *he must have spent years developing that cold politeness.* So he told him about the book and about Toskini's house, the room next door and the person or persons unknown who had been in his room. And he told him about the flowers and the picture and the light.

There was a short silence on the other end of the line, then the lieutenant's voice came back on, and Arlen was encouraged to hear a thread of interest.

"I'm still not really convinced, Mr. Arlen, but I have to admit that what you have told me gives me a little more to think about. We haven't a clue as to why this should be murder, but we haven't closed the case and now we will open it a little wider. I have to warn you, though, if you are right, you had better be very careful. A person who has murdered once won't have much compunction about putting someone else away. Just back off and let us take care of it. You aren't in the best of shape to deal with a murderer."

Arlen agreed fervently and hung up. *He's right,* he thought. *How did I ever get myself involved in this mess?* He wondered even more how to get out of it now that they knew he had seen the book. When he was doing a story he used to enjoy the detective work that went along with it, but this time he wished it would just go away so he could forget about it. Maybe it was because there was no story for him to write, but more likely it was that there was a possibility that he might be the next victim.

Arlen was dozing when he was startled by a knock on his door. He hadn't been up since he had called Lt. Crowder because his legs had hurt so badly. He swung off the bed and grabbed his walker and shuffled over and pulled the door open.

Mia was standing in the doorway frowning at him. "Because of you, the police have been all over our facility this morning, disturbing the staff and the guests. They searched Mrs. Toskini's room and the basement. It's all because of your wild theory that Mrs. Toskini was murdered. We've talked about that. You have no reason to believe that. If you persist, we may have to ask you to leave so you don't disturb our guests anymore."

Arlen thought of Toskini's advice about who our friends are, so he didn't say much. He thought that Mia seemed awfully upset for someone only marginally involved, even as he was. So he kept his peace and let her run down, and then he apologized for causing a disturbance. He could see that she wasn't satisfied, but she shrugged her shoulders, turned and left.

As he sat down on his desk chair, he decided he needed to put his new legs to work. He rummaged in the center desk drawer until he found Stan Toskini's business card and dialed the number.

"Hi, Mr. Toskini. It's Arlen. Got a minute?"

"Hi, Mr. Arlen. How about calling me Stan. What can I do for you?"

"I need your legs and mind for a while, Stan, and please just call me Arlen."

"Okay, Arlen, I volunteer the legs, but I'm not sure about the mind, but go ahead."

"It seems like our front desk lady, Mia Carson, is really concerned about me nosing around here. She may just not want the publicity for Meadowview, but she may have another motive. I'd like you to see if you can snoop around and see where she came from and what she did before she came here."

"Sure, I've got a little slack time. Where do you think I ought to start?"

Arlen chuckled. "Hey, I think up the big strategies, it's up to you to work out the details. Seriously, though, see if you can find her listed in any societies or organizations or such. I'd like to know where she came from and what she's interested in. I'll try and see what I can find out here without making her nervous." After he hung up and lay down on his non-hospital bed he thought about what he had said and wondered how he could find out anything without raising her red flags, especially if she wasn't who she pretended to be.

A knock on the door ended his daydreams. A youngish woman in green scrubs swung open the door and stepped in, pulling a small chrome cart behind her.

"Mr. Arlen, I'm here to change your bed and clean your bathroom," she said, pulling the cart toward the bathroom door.

"Fine," he answered, "but I had better use it first." His problems with his muscles had given him some more embarrassing disabilities.

As he wheeled his walker out of the bathroom he could see that the maid had torn his bed apart and was busily smoothing out a fresh white sheet.

"What's your name?" he said, trying to sound very casual. "I don't remember seeing you before."

"Tammy Velasquez," she answered, smiling back while she pulled the color-coordinated quilt over the bed. "I usually work on the first floor, but Rosalie is sick so we are doubling up."

"Do you work for Mia?"

"Si, yes. She is my supervisor," she replied.

"Is she a good boss?"

She stopped smiling and stared down at the bed. "She's okay. She's a good boss."

"Hey, I'm not trying to get you in trouble. I just wanted to know. Has she been your boss for a long time?"

"No, she only came here about six months ago. There was a man, but he left suddenly and pretty soon she came." She walked quickly to the bathroom, obviously uncomfortable with the questions.

He lifted his walker to the other side of his body, turned and slowly made his way back to the bathroom door. Sticking his head in, he asked, "What was the name of the guy she replaced?"

She turned around, fear shining in her eyes. "Hector Bozeman," she said very softly and quickly spun back around to the shower door.

Arlen didn't know what he had learned, but the name she had whispered rang a distant bell. Not too distant, but he just couldn't pull it out of the dim recesses of his brain.

As he lay back on his bed, Arlen thought, *it sure is funny, a big tough guy like Stan Toskini being a preacher. I always figured that stuff was for little namby-pamby wimps who couldn't make it in the regular world. Like he had heard somewhere, gentle Jesus, meek and mild. Or else they were in it for the big bucks television shows.* He glanced over at his Grandma's Bible. *That sure doesn't sound like a guy who would hang around with a motorcycle gang, but maybe that's why I've got that Bible. I'll have to read up on it, but not today.*

As he lay there, his legs cramping and his back defying him to get into a comfortable position, he began to doubt himself. Maybe she wasn't murdered. Maybe he had just been an Agatha Christie fan for too many years. If an old lady like Mrs. Toskini fell out of bed on her head, she could have broken her neck. That hospital bed of hers should have had side rails on it like they do in real hospitals! Maybe Mia was just being defensive because her company didn't want a lawsuit. But what about the tipped over wheelchair? On that dismal note, he fell asleep.

Arlen didn't know how long he had been asleep, but suddenly he was trying to jump up out of bed and was being stabbed in the back with crushing pain. *Calm down,* he told himself. *Jumping around won't do any good.* The phone buzzed again in the quiet evening. He slowly swung his feet around and placed them firmly on the floor and pulled his walker closer. By now the phone had rung three or four times, and he was afraid they would give up before he got there. Pushing the walker ahead of himself in the dark room, he managed to shove the desk chair over to bang a big mark on the wall before he was able to fumble the phone up to his good ear.

"Arlen here."

"Arlen, its Stan. I hope I didn't wake you up, but I thought you would be interested in what I found out."

"What time has it gotten to be? I fell asleep worrying about this mystery and getting pretty discouraged."

"It's only about 11:00 PM, but I wanted to talk to you before I did any more. I had one of my sharp young computer nerds try and find out something about Mia. He assured me that there is no such person as your Mia Carson. She doesn't exist!"

CHAPTER 5

"Perhaps she has never done anything to get her name on the Internet," Arlen said.

"No, he said that if she is living, or has ever lived, he could find out something about her, if it was only her name and phone number, but he found nothing at all. He found quite a few Mia Carsons, but none that fit her."

"Very interesting. I found out that she has only worked here about six months. How about seeing if your computer guy can find out anything about a man named Hector Bozeman. He left here suddenly about six months ago."

Toskini chuckled grimly. "That's a no brainer for sure. Hector Bozeman is the guy that was found in the lake about six or seven months ago. One of our motorcycle guys found him floating near the boat dock. He was pretty messed up, but they identified him by his DNA. Why did you ask about him?"

"I knew I had heard that name before. Hector Bozeman was the person that was replaced by Mia as the manager of this place. Now I'm beginning to get scared," Arlen said. "I don't think I should have told her so much, she might not be all that innocent."

"Be very careful, my friend. I will keep trying and will drop by tomorrow afternoon and we can compare notes. Keep your door locked, go back to sleep. I'll keep you in my prayers."

"Well, I've thought about getting myself a gun, but if I had one, I'd probably shoot myself in the foot by accident, and then I would have more to worry about than I do now!"

With that piece of unsinkable logic and Toskini's emphatic "no way!" He hung up and lay back down on his bed, but he couldn't go back to sleep. When the body is relaxed, the brain seems to work overtime, and he couldn't stop thinking about Mrs. Toskini.

That was how he spent the night. He just couldn't put together the pieces of what he knew, but he was now absolutely sure it was murder. He wasn't clear about what changed his mind. Before he got the telephone call he was vacillating, but now he was dead sure. He even grinned a little at the pun, until he remembered Mrs. Toskini's frail body lying on the floor. She had been brutally murdered, and it angered him to realize that someone was getting away with it.

At about three thirty am he had to get up and sit in his chair because his back and his legs were screaming at him from all the tossing and turning he did as he had churned the problem over and over.

For the second time in 24 hours he was startled out of a sound sleep the next day. He had come back up from lunch, lay down, and had immediately fallen asleep. He was trying to make up for his bad night, but he jumped at least a foot when Stan banged on the door. Might as well have stayed up, he thought grumpily, as he shuffled over to the door. He had to holler at Stan to wait a minute, because he had taken his advice and locked his door.

As he opened the door he stopped and stared at the man in front of him. His hair was neatly combed, he was wearing a long-sleeved dress shirt and a grey sports coat which hid his tattoos. He looked much more like Arlen's image of a preacher.

"What happened to you, you look almost civilized?"

"This is my alter-ego. I look like this when I'm dealing with the part of the populace that doesn't like us motorcycle riders," he said, as he pulled up the desk chair and plunked down in it.

"Well, you sure look more like my idea of a preacher now."

"Arlen, I think you should drop this thing before you get hurt. I don't know how much help I can give you, and you've already found that someone can get into your room pretty easily. Maybe you ought to move to another place."

"No! I'm not going to let anyone chase me out of here. Besides, I just can't get it out of my mind, and it happened too close to home to ignore. If I thought the police were really investigating it, I would be more apt to leave it alone, but that lieutenant's attitude about the case doesn't inspire any confidence in me." He sighed, shrugged his shoulders, and continued, "Besides, Mia knows I am interested and, if she's on the other side, she might not be able to afford to leave me alone. So far she hasn't said much to me, but I expect she will. I'd sure like to know who she really is." He fell back down on his bed.

"Okay, but don't say I didn't warn you. What would you like for me to do now?"

"Everyone exists. Just because your man couldn't find Mia's name and address doesn't mean that she's invisible. There must be some records of how and why she was hired here. She must have a different name. If your guy is smart enough he can probably hack into the computer that this assisted living company uses for its records. They have more than one location, so they must pass e-mail and stuff back and forth."

"I won't encourage these guys to do stunts that are illegal, but I'll have him try again on the Internet. Give me a day to get him back on it, and we'll see what happens. In the meantime you stay low and don't get into trouble with Mia." He got up and turned toward the door.

"Okay, but I think I'll snoop around here to the best of my limited ability. I just had this thought that they must keep paper records around someplace. I'm not too mobile, but I might be able to find their archives or their storage location. At least I'll be doing something."

After Stan had left, Arlen had what he congratulated himself was a brilliant thought. If his stuff was stored in the basement, their records were probably down there too. He decided it was time to take his walker for a walk.

He had noticed from the buttons that the passenger elevators didn't go below the lobby, so he put 'his little gray cells' (as Christie's Poroit would say) to work and figured out there must be a freight elevator somewhere, probably in the same area. He had never seen them carrying heavy furniture or equipment up or down in the passenger elevators, so he knew a freight elevator must have carried his heavy desk up to the third floor.

As he shuffled down the hall toward the passenger elevators, he noticed a wide wooden door set in the wall near the first elevator. He hadn't paid much attention to it, just assuming it was some sort of storage closet. But now he grabbed the handle, figuring it was locked, and was almost knocked off balance by the ease with which the big door swung open. The wide hollow core door hid a large gray steel elevator door. On the left doorframe two black buttons stuck out. One said 'up', the other 'down'. *Well, down is where I want to go,* he thought, and so he pushed the down button. He glanced quickly up and down the comfortably empty hall, stepped in the big padded car, pressed B and was swooshed down to the basement in no time. As the door slid open, he could see that he was in another world. No pastel paintings, no soft carpets, just gray cement and lots of unpainted plywood.

All along both sides of the wide hallway tan plywood doors stood in uneven rows. Each door was numbered with a room number and each lhad a silver hasp with a Yale lock stuck through it. He rolled his walker clear down to the end of the hallway. At the far wall he ran into a steel door marked FIRE EXIT. Well, he thought, back to square one. He pushed his walker clear to the other end and started down the next hall.

He was already getting pretty tired by this time, with the better part of two halls still to go, but he gritted his teeth and started down the long passage. About two thirds of the way down this hall, the plywood doors ran out, and he saw a real door in the left-hand wall. The sign over the door said: 'Cleaning Supplies'. Then he spied another door just beyond the first one. It looked more promising. A big sign over the green steel door said 'Records'.

He thought, *I can't be lucky enough to find another door unlocked*, but when he twisted the handle the door swung slightly ajar. He pushed it open and shuffled into the big room. He carefully almost closed the door behind him, leaving it ajar, and found the light switch. White fluorescent glow showered the room. He thought how fortunate that was, because there were all sorts of tripping hazards on the floor. Several low step stools were scattered around the room here and there to give access to a group of white cabinets that jutted out over the tops of a gaggle of gray file drawers.

There his luck ran out. All of the white cabinets seemed to be locked and the file cabinets had big round steel bars stuck through the drawer pulls and locked with combination locks. Not very high tech, but effective. He moved down the aisle rattling doors and checking locks with no success and finally ended up clear down at the end of the row.

As he started to turn he heard a small click and realized instantly what it was. Someone had closed the door and snapped the lock. He worked his way back to the door, but it was locked firmly. *Now I'm in a real mess*, he thought. *Mia must have seen me get into the elevator and followed me down. I bet she came down the fire stairs.*

He decided that the first thing he had to do was to find a place to sit down. His legs were almost beyond the limit of their capability, and he was shaking like a leaf. He moved away from the door and tried to lower himself onto one of the step stools, but he immediately fell off onto his side. The pain was excruciating. He straightened his legs as he lay there on the concrete floor, thinking bad thoughts about his snoopy nature. *If only I could have left things alone, I wouldn't be in this mess. I'm really done for this time,* he thought. *Unless someone comes down and looks for some records, I will die on this floor. And I know who would come down here, Mia. I don't suppose she would be too interested in my condition.*

He didn't know if he could get up, but he had to try. He had gotten a little more upper body strength from using his walker, but he still couldn't pull himself up on the step stool. He tried for what seemed like an hour and was utterly wiped out. He finally had to stop and rest. He had never believed much in religion, but right then he was wishing he had asked Toskini a little more about his faith. *This would be a good time to know more about it than I do.* He thought. But while he was pondering God, he fell asleep.

CHAPTER 6

H e didn't know what woke him, but a sound, like a rasp of a rough file on metal, pushed its way into his consciousness. He looked at the door and saw light streaming through a crack that wasn't there before. He crawled and pushed his way over to the door jamb and had to rest again. Finally he pushed himself and his walker against the door and it swung open, making him sprawl out face down on the cement. This time he had the whole hallway to roll around in. Pushing his walker against the door jamb, he managed to get enough leverage to get to his feet. He decided he never wanted to sleep on a concrete floor again.

Now all he had to do was to figure out who it was that had locked him in and even more puzzling, who had let him out. The hallway was still empty, and not even a mouse or a bug moved down the nicely lit passage. He had to say this for them, they kept the place neat and clean.

Back at the elevator door he pushed the button for the first floor, deciding it would be safer to get out of the freight elevator as soon as possible and to take the passenger elevator the rest of the way.

As the door swung open at the first floor, he had a quick second thought, and sure enough his worst fears were realized. Mia was standing there frowning at him.

"Why are you in the freight elevator, Mr. Arlen?"

"I just wondered where my storage area was. Who has the key to it?"

"Mr. Arlen, you aren't in good enough shape to go down to your locker. If you want anything out of it, just ask us."

"I certainly will, next time. It is very interesting down there, as I'm sure you know."

"Yes, I often have to go down there, but we don't encourage our guests to do it since it isn't fixed up nicely like the rest of the building. Please don't go down there again." She waved toward the freight elevator, turned on her heel and strode off down the hall.

Arlen had once thought that he might like to get to know her better, but today had changed his mind. She might be pretty deadly.

Back in his room, he had to call the therapist to help him take a bath and change his clothes. Arlen fought having to have help, and most of the time was still able to fend for himself, but sometimes the muscle part of his problem was more severe and so overcame his aversion to asking for help. Ben came with his smile and it was soon over.

"Ben. How come you are into that religious stuff?"

"I'm not into any religious stuff, Mr. Arlen. I'm a Christian."

"But man, you're a big strong guy able to take care of yourself. I'd expect it more of a weak wimpy guy like me."

Ben smiled at him and said, "You certainly could use my Lord. But just because I'm strong doesn't mean I don't need help. And my Jesus gives me the kind of help I can't get anyplace else. You should try it."

"Stan keeps telling me the same thing. He must have some angle, don't you think? Why would anyone run around the state trying to sell religion unless there was something in it for them?"

"There is a whole lot in it for him, Mr. Arlen. He gets the best satisfaction of all. He gets to know that he has led someone from the depths of hell into eternal life."

"Wow. That's something to think about, if I believed in eternal life. But that's just part of the gimmick. Nobody really believes that stuff."

"I do."

"Well, I'll have to think about it some. I have been meeting a lot of strong young people like you who believe it all. So it seems like it might be worth researching it a bit. But now, I've got to go to bed. Thanks for your great help."

"Read your Bible and talk to God, Mr. Arlen. And if you have any questions I'd be glad to talk to you. It's my favorite subject."

Later as Arlen lay on his bed, he tried and tried to figure out what had happened. He could understand someone locking him in the room, but for the life of him, he couldn't figure out why someone would let him out. And especially would let him out and not come in to see if he was all right. He went to sleep with the puzzle rattling around in his head. With his brain so active and his body sore, he didn't sleep very well and was glad when morning came.

With the dawn came the thought: *I've been entirely too wrapped up in Mrs. Toskini and I think I need a little change of pace.*

When he came back from breakfast he spied a brightly colored notice on the bulletin board across the hall. He shuffled over and stared at it. In large blue and red letters it invited everyone on the third floor to a little get together right in their area, starting just before lunch.

It seemed like a pretty good deal to him, so at eleven o'clock he was on his way to the meeting room, which was on the opposite side of the hall from the weight room and the library.

The double doors to the room were open and he was disconcerted to find Mia standing in the middle of the opening. But she just smiled at him and said, "Welcome, Mr. Arlen, I'm glad you have decided to mix in with the other guests.

Perhaps it will take your mind off of things you shouldn't be thinking about." She stepped aside and motioned toward the room. "Come on in."

He said, "I hope you are right, I really need to be able to sleep better at night."

"All of these people live on your floor, and you should get to know them. I'm sure there are some that you can share common interests with."

Arlen walked past her and entered the room. He thought, *meeting rooms sure are the same all over the world.* This one had a bunch of five-foot round folding tables surrounded by brown metal folding chairs. He could see that many were already crowding around the big coffee urn that sat on a table by the door of a small kitchen. A few others were seated in scattered locations throughout the room. Altogether he decided there must have been about twenty people there.

Mia closed the doors and walked back toward the coffeepot. She picked up a small black wireless microphone from the coffee table and said, "Everyone find a seat and we'll get started."

This started a small stampede toward the tables, except for the two or three who decided that getting coffee was more important than getting started. He opted to get his coffee later and pulled up a chair to a table as near to the door as he could get. He figured that way he could bug out if the thing got as boring as he figured it might.

"I'm happy you all decided to come today. The only way you will be able to live a more normal life is to get to know your neighbors and to work and play together. So we have these monthly meetings to introduce new residents and hopefully to learn something interesting about each other. I am going to call on each of you to make a little speech. Now those who are new don't get nervous. I would just like each of you to say your name, where you came from and anything else that might help your neighbors to get to know you."

One by one, the men and women got up, or sat in their wheelchairs, and spoke their little piece. Arlen was impressed to find that each of these frail, old-looking people had really been somebody at one time. That little gray-haired lady, for example, couldn't have been over four feet tall, but she had been a missionary in the south of Mexico for 45 years. He learned later that she had seen several of her sisters in the mission raped and murdered by rebels and had lost her husband there twenty years ago. She was still bright and coherent and he thought she would be a good person to know. As a journalist, he had never gone in for interviewing religious people or writing stories about them, but he was beginning to realize that some people really lived the stuff for some reason he thought he might like to figure out. Perhaps this woman could tell him what he was missing.

By the time it came to his turn he was truly ashamed of his bitterness and sorrow at his affliction. He had been sure that he had gotten about the rawest deal to come down the pike, but none of these people wanted to be here or to need this kind of help, and many were in much worse physical condition than he was.

He was the last one and after he had finished, Mia told them that he was the newest guest on the third floor and everyone applauded. Then a pale little lady sitting at the next table said, "I feel I know you already, Mr. Arlen. I have read your column in The Journal for years. You are a wonderful writer."

Arlen couldn't help but bask in the glow of the compliments and suddenly the place didn't look so bad, and he decided it would be nice to get to know them all better. While getting his coffee, he also met a lady named Betsy who had been Mrs. Toskini's neighbor on the other side. He decided they would have to do some serious talking.

The program progressed and soon it was one o'clock and time for lunch. This break gave him a little time to talk to Betsy.

"Yes, I heard Rose crying and that wasn't the first time. I'd been terribly worried about her for some time."

"Why is that?"

"She didn't seem the same. She was always worried about something, I don't know what."

"Did you ever see her big address book?" Arlen asked.

"Yes, she had a lot of names in that book. She even had some funny symbols beside some of the names, but she never told me what they meant."

Then she had a puzzler for him. "Have they made you sign over your property yet?" she asked in her soft voice.

"What do you mean?"

"Well, sooner or later they put a lot of pressure on you to sign over any property you might have to them to guarantee that you can pay for your room until you die."

"That doesn't sound too legal."

"I know that Rose was really worried about it because she didn't have any property, and she thought they might throw her out. I thought the symbols might have something to do with who had been contacted, but I'm not sure."

"Did she try and look into who had and who hadn't signed over their property?" he asked.

"Oh yes, she was a mystery fan, especially Miss Marple stories, and she was excited about solving a real mystery." Betsy suppressed a little sob and then smiled, "I really liked her. We got to be good friends."

"How long have you lived here, Betsy?" It was a reporter's question.

"Oh, I've been here about a year".

"How about Mrs. Toskini?"

"I think Rose had been here about five or six years. She seemed happy most of the time. Now she's gone and I miss her." She turned her head away but Arlen thought he saw a tear on her pale cheek.

Pretty soon it was over and he was surprised to find that he had enjoyed himself. Betty wasn't beautiful, but she sure was pleasant to be around.

So they have ulterior motives, he thought as he lay in his bed later that night. *They not only want my monthly payments, they also want everything I have.* He went to sleep wondering why they hadn't contacted him yet.

CHAPTER 7

I t hadn't been long in coming though. The next morning, before he had even managed to pull himself out of bed, he heard a loud knock on his door.

"Hang on, I'm still in bed," he hollered at the door.

There was no answer, so he swung himself slowly out of his bed and grabbed his walker. He figured that anyone who came around that early in the morning deserved to see him in his pajamas, so he didn't even bother to put on his robe. That was a job in itself and better not tried early in the day.

He opened the door to a tall dark man he had never seen before. He was wearing an expensive Italian designer suit and obviously had a better barber than Arlen did in old Pete, who had trimmed his thinning hair for years.

Right away he didn't like this man. *Sometimes*, he thought, *you just look at a person and he gets under your skin*. It was that way with this guy, and from the look of his muscled body, he could be capable of breaking a person's kneecaps if he wasn't happy.

"Mr. Arlen, my name is Devon and I am a property manager for Meadowview. I would like to come in and talk to you for a few minutes." With that he brushed Arlen aside and strode into the room.

"Make yourself right at home." But Arlen saw the sarcasm was wasted and went and sat on his bed.

45

"I'll come right to the point, Mr. Arlen. We know that most of the people that come to live with us are not well endowed financially. So we have provided a plan whereby you can guarantee that you will be able to live here the rest of your life. Do you own a home?"

"No, I sold it when I moved in here. Why?"

"Do you own any other kind of property?"

Arlen stood up and faced the man. "Look, you may have heard, we old crocks can get pretty grumpy, so if you have a point, please make it!"

"Mr. Arlen, it doesn't help anything for you to get belligerent." The man said it without a trace of expression on his face. Now that Arlen was standing in front of him and he could look into his steely gray eyes, the thought flashed through his mind, *this is a man who could break a little old lady's neck.*

But he kept his cool and said, "I just don't like beating around the bush. It you have some kind of a plan, let me know and I will tell you if I am interested."

"If that's the way you want it, here it is. We have lots of people waiting for a chance to move in here. If we believe you will be unable to keep paying for your room, we will have no choice but to move you out and give the space to someone else. Now do you have any property or not?" His face could have been a model for a statue. Only his lips moved.

"I have a little property, but I'm not inclined to get rid of it right now, and I believe that as long as I am paying the bill you will have a difficult time getting rid of me."

"Our attorneys have gotten around that obstacle rather nicely, Mr. Arlen." Devon actually smiled a little. "You may not have noticed when you signed into this place, but it is for people who are still mostly able to take care of themselves. And the fine print in that contract also says that we are the ones to make that decision." The smile was gone into the blankness of his face. "So all we have to do is to say that we don't feel that you are able to take care of yourself and you are out of here. Seems pretty simple to me."

Arlen shuddered as he thought about being kicked out of Meadowview. He knew that most good places had long waiting lists. But he pushed his walker over to the door, swung it open, and through grim lips said, "This conversation is over, whatever your name is. Now please leave. I can only take so much garbage at a time, and I am pretty full up now."

The man slowly rose from the guest chair and faced him. Arlen noticed again how broad he was in the shoulders.

"Perhaps you had better think about it, Mr. Arlen, nice places like this aren't easy to get into. Meadowview is a very fine complex, as I'm sure you have found out, and all we ask is that we are assured of a continued method of payment from you as time passes.

"Goodbye, I will think about it, but right now I am not in the mood, so go away!"

As soon as the door closed, Arlen lost his bravado, and he couldn't stop from shaking. He was sure the man's bite was every bit as bad as his bark. But he was blessed if they were going to take his little piece of Arizona property that he had hung onto for years. He didn't even remember why he had bought it, and he had only seen it once or twice, but now it felt like the most important thing he owned. He smiled to himself – it was actually the only thing he owned, and he would rather give it to George and his boys than to have it coerced away from him.

He had barely made it back to his bed when there was a soft knock on his door. "Come in, it isn't locked."

He was surprised to find Mia standing in the doorway. She smiled and said, "May I come in?"

"Sure, your partner was just here. You might as well go ahead and completely ruin my day. And I haven't even had breakfast yet. I get this way when I am awakened too early."

"I'm sorry, Mr. Arlen, I really want to be your friend. We seem to have gotten off on the wrong foot with each other over Mrs. Toskini's death. Let's try and forget that and start over. I want your stay here to be pleasant. This is a nice place, as I'm sure you have already found out, and we want you to be happy."

It was a long speech and he began to wonder if he was wrong about her, but then he remembered his previous visitor and took it out on her.

"That's pretty hard, considering the threats your bully boy made to me a few minutes ago. I'm sure his whole approach is illegal, but most of the guests here don't have the contacts or the power to fight you. But I think I might try. I still have a few contacts in the city, and some of them owe me a favor."

"Please don't do that, Mr. Arlen. Mr. Devon isn't someone to mess around with." She sat down in the guest chair. As he had noticed before, she was a very beautiful young woman with her dark hair framing her healthy tanned face, and he noticed again how she lit up when she smiled. But he was still upset, so he said, "I just don't want to be pressured into something I don't think is right." He thought as he said it, *what a whiner I have turned out to be.*

"Just go along with Mr. Devon for a little while. It will be much easier on all of us. He might not be here much longer. And don't forget your doctor's appointment." She smiled again and got up and was out the door before he could put his foot into his mouth again. He couldn't help noticing, though, how smoothly and gracefully she moved, almost with no effort. She had learned somewhere how to be well coordinated.

As he pulled himself over to his desk, he glanced at his calendar, and realized that his doctor's appointment was in only about two hours. He had forgotten it since they had called and changed the date and time because the doctor had gone out of town. *Must be a golf tournament somewhere*, he thought. No, he shouldn't be so sarcastic. Dr. Nelson was a good doctor and had helped him a lot. It was just that it was hard to get in to see him, and even when you did have an appointment it took forever to actually get examined. Mia had scheduled the hospital express car to come for him, and now he was sitting in the Meadowview lobby waiting impatiently to be picked up. The problem was that he wasn't much of a waiter. One of his readers, when he had found out Arlen had this serious disease, had written to him and told him that the Bible said, "They who wait on the Lord will renew their strength." He was still waiting. And he still hadn't looked at his Grandma's Bible. He'd have to do that one day.

The volunteer driver showed up nearly on time and, as he helped Arlen get into the car, Arlen stared at him. He was a cheerful old guy, at least ten years older than Arlen. *That's a laugh*, he thought, *here I am a relatively young man and being driven around by an old crock*. Then he decided he was glad for the ride and sat back and relaxed as the man expertly worked his way through the heavy traffic and got him to the doctor's office fifteen minutes before his appointment time.

The older man opened the door for Arlen and said, "Can I get you a wheelchair?"

That upset him, too. *Here is this old guy offering to wheel me around in a wheelchair*. He frowned and said, "No," and started to shuffle off toward the lobby of the two story medical building. When the volunteer saw how bull-headed Arlen was being, he got back in his car and started to drive off. Arlen could swear he saw him laugh and then put his hand up to cover his smile. *I've just got to learn to accept help*, he thought. He navigated his way into the doctor's waiting room, checked in with Pam at the little window and was waiting again. As he surveyed the room, he thought, *I've never been in the middle of China, but I'll bet the waiting rooms are the same, even there*. One thing he noticed though, was that

49

the chairs had improved. The chairs in Dr. Nelson's waiting room were a step or two above the old ones, but after waiting almost an hour, his back was still complaining bitterly.

Finally the nurse pushed the door open and called his name, then waited patiently while he pulled himself up and got his walker going in the right direction and slowly made his way past her and through the open door.

"Hi, Mr. Arlen. Nice to see you again. Let's get weighed, shall we?"

She was such a nice young nurse that he bit his tongue and didn't offer his usual witticism, "sorry there's not room enough for both of us on that scale." He stepped on the scale and found that he had lost five more pounds. That wasn't good, and the doctor was still trying to figure out exactly why he was losing weight. It was just another little puzzle he didn't know how to answer.

He was led into a small square room, full of a chrome and black examining table and white wall cabinets. The walls on both sides were covered with pictures of dogs and cats. He thought, *wow, maybe the doctor is a vet.* There were two old magazines on the table and Arlen rested his arm on them as the young nurse pulled the blood pressure cuff from the wall bracket and wrapped it around his arm. She wrote on his chart then punched something into the small laptop she carried and then got up and opened the door.

"The doctor will be in to see you in a few minutes," she said with a smile and then turned and walked out and closed the door.

Finally the door opened and Dr. Nelson ambled in. Arlen had a lot of faith in him because he always seemed to tell him the straight stuff, no matter how hard it was to take. He had been the one who had recommended Meadowview.

Dr. Nelson pulled the small roll-around stool over to the table and sat down and began punching the screen of his laptop with a small plastic rod.

"Doc, what do you know about Meadowview?"

"It is highly recommended by most of the discharge planners. I've heard that the food is good and they take pretty good care of their residents. Why?"

So Arlen told him of his encounter with Devon and how if he didn't do what they wanted he would probably be looking for a new residence.

"That sounds pretty shady. I have never heard about that before. It really makes it difficult for you, because we don't have too many good places for people to go in this city. Some of the big corporations are building places, but many of them are so concerned with the bottom line that they aren't too pleasant to live in."

"Don't I know it? If I get kicked out of Meadowview, I don't know what I will do. I don't have many options. But I'm not going to give them my little piece of property, even if I have to move. I don't like being pushed around!"

The doctor examined him and said he was about the same, but that he had a brand new medication he wanted Arlen to try. He thought it would help him to put some weight back on and could relieve the terrible muscle cramps he often had.

It wasn't an altogether good visit, but he was pleased that he didn't seem to be any worse than he had been three months ago, except for the weight loss. The doctor had said, "Mr. Arlen, you are just going to have to eat more. That's not advice I often give to my patients, but I can't see the reason why you are still losing weight. Try eating some snacks between meals." He laughed and said, "I never thought I'd give anyone that kind of advice, I'll be tossed out of the AMA, but you can't afford to lose much more weight."

Arlen had gotten his prescription and had been waiting for another boring hour for the hospital express to pick him up, but he didn't make a fuss, because he had been told that they only had a few volunteers to drive everyone around. He had never made any kind of an effort to help his fellow citizens

51

very much, so he felt guilty about accepting rides from others. This time the driver was a gruff gray-haired lady who didn't talk much but got him back to Meadowview quickly and in one piece.

Just as he had shuffled through the main entrance and past the real live trees in the Meadowview lobby, he heard, "Hey, Mr. Arlen."

He jumped and looked back at the desk and saw Lt. Crowder talking to Mia.

Crowder motioned for him to stay put and quickly walked over to where he stood.

"Can we go up to your room and talk a little?" he said, quite humbly for him.

"Sure, what's new, Lieutenant?"

"I'd like to wait until we get up to your room, Mr. Arlen, I don't like to discuss things out in the hall." By this time they were at the elevators, and neither of them said anything until they were in his room with the door closed. Lt. Crowder sat down heavily in the guest chair and Arlen fell down in his usual place on his bed.

"Mr. Arlen, I want to apologize for not paying more attention to you when you said that Mrs. Toskini was murdered. It just didn't seem to add up at the time, but now it seems much more likely."

"Why, what happened?"

"Do you know her grandson, Stanley?"

"Sure, he seems to be a swell guy. We have been sort of cooperating on trying to figure this thing out." Arlen looked at him suspiciously, "Why, what happened?"

"He called us and told us he had found some sort of notebook or address book that you and he were looking for, and he was going to bring it in yesterday and show it to me. He never showed up. So this morning I was in the area and dropped in on him. He wasn't there. His guys told me he had been beaten to a pulp. It was touch and go for a while, but they think he will live. He is in the hospital in the critical care unit. He hasn't been able to talk to tell us what happened, but I know that there was no notebook or address book in his place, and it had been pretty badly messed up."

"Oh no!! I wonder where he got that book. I know some of the people he works with walk pretty close to the line, maybe they found it for him. Boy, I wish I could get down to the hospital and see him!"

"Well, he can't see anyone right now, but if you'd like, I'll come by and pick you up and we will go see him as soon as they let us. In the meantime, I suppose you have ignored my fatherly advice and gone and messed in this case. Have you found out anything?"

"I know these Meadowview people aren't as innocent as we have been led to think. They are trying to strong-arm me out of my only little piece of property. They have a very nasty type named Devon who laid it on me pretty good yesterday. Our friend Mia defended him, saying he might not be here much longer. So I suppose she is in on it too."

"I told you before, be careful. You aren't in a position to fight these guys. We don't know who is on our side and who is on theirs. I'd be much happier if you just let us do our jobs. But in any case, be careful!" With that profound bit of advice, he pulled himself up out of the chair and headed for the door. "I'll give you a call when we can go see Toskini." He pulled open the door and strode out.

CHAPTER 8

A rlen lay back on his bed and picked up his jangling phone. "Arlen here."

"Hi, Unc. It's George. I just wondered how you were doing. Beth and I just got more or less settled in our new house. Things sure are different here in Minnesota."

"How's your job going? Have they made you president of the company yet?"

George laughed. "This is a huge international company. I am going to have to get used to being a very small cog in a very big wheel. I have to tell you, I'm not sure I'm going to like it."

"You'll get used to it. If you don't, you guys can come back out here. I miss you already."

"Are you getting settled in pretty well? I expect you are getting used to the quiet. No big stories to drive you insane. It must be a real blessing. I wish I was retired."

"Say, there is more excitement here than there was in the newspaper business. My next door neighbor was murdered, and some tough guy is trying to force me to give up my little Arizona property that I want to leave to you and your kids. Someone locked me in the storage room. Lucky someone saw it and let me out. It has been very interesting."

There was a long pause. "Are you serious? What kind of a place did I get you in to? Hang on a minute."

In the background he heard, "Beth! Come here, quick." Then low voices, too soft for him to understand. Then finally George came back on the line and said, "I'll be out there tomorrow. I need to get you out of that place. Maybe we can bring you back here. This is pretty nice country."

Arlen hollered, "No! You're just getting settled down. There is no reason for you to come here. I've got everything under control. Stay home!"

"I can't do that. I got you into this mess, I'll get you out. Just hang on until I get there. Beth has already made my reservations."

"George, I don't want you to come here. What about your job? They won't think lightly of you leaving right after you got there. They might fire you."

"Look, Unc, let me worry about that. My plane gets in about three PM, so I should be there about four. Tell them I'll be there for dinner. Gotta go pack. Bye." The phone clicked.

Arlen pounded his hand on the bed and sighed. *I never could tell that boy anything. What in the world am I going to do now?* Arlen picked up the phone and called Mia.

"Meadowview. This is Mia."

"Hi Mia, this is Arlen. I just want to warn you that my family is mad at Meadowview and George is coming out from Minnesota to fix everything."

"What in the world are you talking about Mr. Arlen? Why would George be mad at us?"

"I made the mistake of telling him what has been going on around here, and he is ready to pack me off to a funny farm in Minnesota. So I need your help."

"I'll do anything I can. Is your nephew always this precipitous?"

"I didn't think so, but he thinks he got me into a mess and that it is his duty to get me out. It isn't."

"What can I do?"

"I couldn't stop him from coming, but I figure if we both talk sense into him he will go back to Minnesota and mind his own business."

"He's only trying to protect you. But I see your point. I will help all I can. We can get together in my office and talk. Just bring him down when he comes in."

"Thanks, I don't know what else to do. As you say, he is only trying to protect me. The problem is that I was protecting myself long before he was born. I'll let you know when he gets here."

The next afternoon as Arlen was watching the afternoon news, his door rattled. "Come on in, George, it isn't locked."

George pushed open the door and rushed into the room. "Are you okay?"

"George, I'm fine. You shouldn't have come."

"Are you sure you're okay?"

"Calm down George. What in the world are you doing wasting your money flying out here? You know I can take care of myself."

George flopped down in Arlen's desk chair. "It didn't sound like it to me when you called. Your neighbor was murdered, people getting locked up in airless rooms and them threatening to throw everybody out if you don't give them your property. What's goin' on?"

Arlen sighed. "It wasn't an airless room. They have very good ventilation. Let's go down and talk to Mia. Maybe she can help you sort this out." He stood up and grabbed his walker.

"Huh! She must be part of the problem. Why should I talk to her?"

"Get off your rear and come on. I'm losing my patience. I just thought that she could talk a little sense into your thick head."

They took the elevator down to the first floor. Mia was at the front desk checking someone in. She looked up and smiled, and said, "Go on into my office. I will be there when I am through with this gentleman. Ben can take him up to his room." She nodded back in the direction of her office. She picked up the phone and as they walked off they heard her say, "Ben?"

They had been sitting in Mia's office for only a few minutes when George stomped his foot on the floor and stared at the door. "I might have known she wasn't interested in talking to us. Where the blazes is she?"

"We've only been here ten minutes. She's got other things to do than to talk to us. It takes a few minutes to check someone in..."

The office door burst open and Mia rushed in.

"Sorry. Our new resident has some special needs and that took a few minutes." She walked around her desk and slid into her office chair. "Now, Mr. Arlen – George – what is bothering you?"

George sputtered, "What's bothering me? You got someone murdered. Someone is strong arming Unc for his Arizona property. How do I know that he won't be the next one to be murdered? How often does this stuff happen? I mean, this is ridiculous." He waved his arms in agitation.

Arlen reached over and pulled his arm down and said, "George, I told you to calm down. Mia isn't the enemy. She just wants to know what has got you so upset that you felt you had to fly 2000 miles to set it straight."

"Beth's already got a line on a place back in Minneapolis. You can move there this week. As far as I know they have never had any murders!"

Arlen smiled at Mia and said, "Please excuse our family feud, but I have to set this young man straight...if I can." He faced George and said, "Now get this straight. I know that you and Beth want to look after me, but I have *no* intention of leaving Meadowview, I *am not* moving to Minneapolis, fine city though it undoubtedly is, and finally, we are trying very

58

hard to avoid getting anyone else murdered, especially me. So go home and see if you can keep from being fired from your new job that you rushed away from without any excuse."

"Well, I'm sorry that you think that I'm being stupid to want to keep you alive. But, I got you into this place and I want to get you to some place that doesn't have people falling over dead every five minutes! If you are back in Minneapolis I can keep an eye on you and help you when you need it without having to jump on an airplane to get to you. Now, come on back upstairs and start packing your stuff. I'll help you. We could leave tomorrow."

Arlen turned to Mia and said, "Can you talk some sense into this guy? I'm about to get mad, and I really don't want to be angry at him. But this is impossible."

Mia nodded, and then looked at George and said, "Mr. Arlen, I can see that you are really upset, and we are too. In spite of your fears this is not something that happens regularly at Meadowview. It is normally a very peaceful and safe place. We have been cooperating with the police, and they are working very hard on the case. I am working equally as hard on the situation of the man who is demanding your uncle's property. It is somewhat of a mystery to me now, but, as I say, I am working on it. I don't know what else we can do. I think your uncle is as safe here as he would be anyplace. Perhaps safer, since the police are watching us rather closely."

"None of that is going to keep Unc from being murdered! I want to talk to the police. Who can I talk to?"

Mia looked at Arlen and then said, "Probably Lt. Crowder would be the best. He knows the facts and I believe that he is in charge of the case."

George jumped out of his chair and yelled, "Where can I find this Crowder guy. I want to talk to him today!"

"He's a busy man, George. He may not be able to talk to you today. Besides, he can't tell you any more than I have already told you. Why don't you just go home?"

George paced the floor between them. "Okay, I'll get a hotel room and see him as soon as I can. I'm not going home until I get this thing solved."

Arlen laughed grimly. "I certainly hope you can solve it. Nobody else seems to be able to. Can't I talk you into leaving it to us? We are doing fine, and as Mia said, everyone is being careful. Go home!"

George rushed out of the room and down the hall. They could hear him on his cell phone calling for a taxi. Arlen turned to Mia and said, "I'm sorry for my volatile relative. I don't know what's gotten into him. I hope he doesn't stir things up. I'm sorry I even mentioned it to him. I was just telling Stan Toskini the other day that I talk too much."

Mia smiled and said, "Yes, I wish you hadn't told him. He could gum up the works if he stirs the pot too much. Not only that but he could put himself in danger. I hope you or Lt. Crowder can talk him into just going home. I will call the lieutenant as soon as we are through here."

Arlen shrugged his shoulders, stood up, and grabbed his walker. "Well, this has worn me out. I'm going upstairs and take a nap. Maybe he will be gone long enough so that I can get a little rest. Thanks for listening to our problems. I appreciate your help."

Mia waved to him as he walked out of the door and said, "Any time."

Arlen was still sleeping an hour later when George pounded on his door and burst into the room. "Okay, I got hold of that lieutenant. He will be here in about an hour. He didn't sound too enthusiastic. You sure he's a good cop?"

"Are you going to spend much more time going around and stirring up my peace and quiet? I talk to Lt. Crowder regularly. He's a busy man. And, yes, I think he is a good cop."

They had just walked back from dinner when Lt. Crowder pounded on the door. Arlen hollered, "Come on in. Join the madhouse."

The lieutenant opened the door and strode in, a frown on his face. "What was so important that you had to call me out of my usually peaceful day?"

George leaped to his feet and said, "What are you doing about keeping my uncle safe? I'm trying to get him to move out of here and come back to Minnesota. Don't you agree with me?"

Arlen smiled and waved his hand at George and said, "This is my excitable nephew, George Arlen. He thinks I am in a hotbed of crime, and that he had to fly all the way out here to rescue me. Will you pour some sense into his worried head?"

"Maybe it would be a good idea for you to go away. It would certainly make my life easier!" Arlen jumped up and started to speak, but the lieutenant held up his hand and said, "I was joking. Sorry. I can see George is really worried. What I would tell you, George, is that your uncle is well established here and comfortable in his life, restricted though it may be. I see no threat that is serious enough to cause him to have to move clear across the country. We are trying very hard to solve the mystery of Mrs. Toskini's death and some other sort of weird things, but I believe we have it covered."

Arlen waved at George to sit down. The young man plunked down in the desk chair and shook his head. "I just don't understand it, this place had such a good reputation. How could these things happen here? Wouldn't it help if he left?"

Lt. Crowder answered, "It's up to him, but I don't think he needs to rush off. If he goes to Minnesota he might get run over by a snowmobile."

"Boy, you're not much help. I flew all the way out here to make sure Unc was safe. You don't make me feel too comfortable about it. Is there someone else in the police department that I can talk to? I'm not going home to I get this figured out."

"Sure. You can talk to my captain, but he will tell you the same thing. We talk about the case every day and he feels exactly the same as I do. It's just a matter of time before we collar the guys who are causing all the trouble."

"Go home, George," Arlen growled.

"Okay, okay, I'll snoop around for another day, and I'll talk to your captain and some people from Meadowview, and if I don't find anything I'll go home and see if I can salvage my job."

"Please don't interfere in this case, Mr. Arlen. These things are very delicate and you could screw things up by nosing around where you don't know what you are doing." Lt. Crowder stood up. "Why don't you do what your uncle says and go home? We've got things under control here."

George jumped up and rushed to the door. "I'll be back tomorrow, Unc. I'm going to snoop around some. I won't cause any trouble." He pulled the door open and rushed out.

"Sorry about that, Lieutenant. I shoulda kept my big mouth shut. It's all my fault."

"That's okay, Mr. Arlen, we all have relatives that give us a pain. You should hear my sister-in-law go on about policemen sometimes. I'll see you later." He followed George out of the door.

George had no sooner left than Arlen's phone jangled on his bedside table. "Arlen here."

"Hi Uncle Arlen. It's Beth. Are you about ready to come back here with us? I've got a lovely spot all picked out."

Arlen sighed and said, "Thanks for your concern, Beth, but I'm not coming back there. I am perfectly happy here and I wish George hadn't come. He is running around like a maniac and is just upsetting a lot of people."

"But he thought you were in deadly danger. Aren't you?"

"No, I'm not. There are some strange things going on here, but the police and the Meadowview folks have it under control. I'm fine. Please don't worry about me."

"Well, all right, if you're sure. This was a real nice place I found, but I understand that you don't want to move. Tell George to come on home. Have him give me a call."

"Thanks a lot, Beth. You seem to have much more sense than your wild husband. But I appreciate that he cares enough to come all the way out here. I hope he doesn't have trouble with his new job because of it. And by the way, I have told him at least ten times to go home. He is out now doing who knows what, and if he keeps harassing the police department he might be out here for quite a while. He is a loose cannon to them and could really mess up their investigation."

He heard Beth's tinkling laugh. "He always was a charger. Sounds like he needed to get a few more facts before he jumped into the fray. Have him call me as soon as possible and I will calm him down. I love you, Uncle Arlen and I'm really glad you are okay."

After Arlen hung up he flopped back on his bed and chuckled to himself. *I wonder how those two ever got together. Oops, I think I introduced them.*

CHAPTER 9

A rlen began to wonder if he had misled Lt. Crowder. His new friend, who had been his legs, had been beaten up and left to die. *I guess his God didn't help him after all,* he thought. He began to wonder, and not for the first time, why he was getting involved in this mystery at all. Maybe the lieutenant was right. Maybe he should chuck it all and then call Devon and tell him he gave up and just go with the flow. *Baloney!* He thought. *No way could I do that.* He flopped back on his bed and thought, *that new medicine must be working already, I'm getting downright hungry!*

Mealtime at his new home was a mixed blessing. The food was excellent, and he didn't know how he would eat if it weren't for the big dining hall on the first floor; but he had to eat when the food was ready, whether he was hungry or not. Most of the time he was not really that excited about eating, but hopefully with his new meds he might even be hungry occasionally –- like now.

Arlen looked around and found an empty spot next to where Betsy was sitting. She smiled at him as he shuffled up beside her and she held his chair as he plopped down into it.

"Hi, Mr. Arlen, how are you today?" He hadn't had anyone brighten his day with such a simple greeting since his wife got sick.

"I'm doing pretty well, Betsy, but why don't you call me Arlen. Mr. Arlen is my father."

"Okay, Arlen. My goodness, here is our food already." She turned and watched as an apron-clad young lady bent over to set a steaming tureen of soup on the table between them.

"Clam chowder today. New York style, nice and hot," the young server said with a smile before she turned and rushed off.

"Well, Betsy, you sure were right. I had my visit from Devon." He noticed her sudden frown. "He looked like the sort of guy who would cheerfully break my nose if I gave him any sass!"

"Oh, I hope you didn't!" The frown deepened. "He is not a nice person."

"I ended up throwing him out of my room, but I am still in one piece." He smiled his macho smile. He knew it didn't fool anyone, but it made him feel better.

"Oh Arlen, be careful. I don't think you should have done that. He won't let up on you and that scares me." She put her hand on his arm and her warm touch made him smile.

"Well, I left myself an out. I told him I would think about it. My little piece of property may not be worth much, but I don't want to be forced into giving it to some yahoo like him!"

"It's just not worth it. If you are going to stay here, you don't need property. Let him have it."

The rest of the dinner was kind of a downer for him after her urgent plea, but he managed to enjoy the braised salmon and fresh asparagus. For dessert they served a homemade berry pie.

He had just returned to his room and sat down when the phone rang. He was sitting on his bed, so he picked it up on the first ring.

"Arlen here." He couldn't quite get over answering the way he had for so many years on the job.

"Hi Arlen. I guess you have heard about my little mishap." The weak voice sounded miles away.

"Stan, how are you doing? Lt. Crowder told me about your set-to. He also told me he would bring me over to see you as soon as you could talk. Does he know you are conscious?"

"No, I have only been coherent for a little while. But I just wanted to tell you that I am all right. I'm worried though. Some of my gang members are pretty mad. They think the guy I got the notebook from set me up. I need someone to talk to them and tell them that it wasn't him. The guys we are going against are just too smart for us. Would it be okay if a couple of them came over to your place and you tried to talk some sense into them?"

Arlen heard in the phone's background, "Rev, Rev, no more talking." He chuckled and said, "Sure, I'll be glad to talk to them if you think it will help. Where are they?"

"They are right outside my door. They haven't left me since it happened. I'll send Rocks and Toby right over. I've got to go. I think I'm going to pass out." He heard voices in the background and then a click as someone hung up the phone.

Arlen decided he had better call down to the front desk and tell the night girl that he was expecting some unusual guests. You had to do that late in the evening, because Meadowview tried to be a pretty secure place after suppertime. People couldn't just walk in.

Then he figured he had better lie down and rest for a while before they came. Stan had been great about the hospital bed and other stuff, and he had finally gotten it moved into his room, and the bed was adjusted just the way he wanted it. He was sure he would be able to rest awhile, because Stan would have to regain consciousness before he could send his men over.

He had just fallen asleep when there was a loud pounding on his door. He glanced at his clock, surprised at how fast they had gotten there and then hollered, "Come in. Don't break it down!"

Two very big dudes squeezed themselves through the open door. The first one was about six four and had very broad shoulders bulging out from under a black leather motorcycle jacket. He carried a small black skull helmet under his left arm. Behind him the other man was almost as tall, but not nearly so wide. In fact he looked skinny when compared with the first man. He was all dressed in faded blue denim, from his tight jeans to his shirt with the little orange tab on the pocket, to a stiff jacket with W.W.J.D. embroidered over the pocket

"Mr. Arlen?" the first one growled.

"That's me. You Rocks or Toby?"

"I'm Rocks, that's Toby." He jerked his thumb over his shoulder.

"Well, come in and sit if you can find a chair that will hold you. How is Stan doing?"

"He pretty near bought it this time," Toby said, settling down in the small guest chair. Rocks plopped down in the desk chair and Arlen went back and sat on his bed, adjusting it up to support his back.

"He was about to pass out when he talked to me on the phone. Did he come to?"

"Oh yeah, he is just on a lot of pain medication and it gets to him occasionally. He is one tough guy."

Arlen looked hard at Toby. "What do you mean this time? Has this happened before?"

Toby gave him a pitying look like he was simple minded. "Look, Mr. Arlen, Rev is working with a bunch of the toughest people in this country. Some of them resent him trying to straighten them out. This is at least the third time he has ended up in the hospital. But this was different. Whoever did this was very professional at beating a man to death. If it hadn't been Rev he would be dead now. As Rocks said, he is one tough guy. He said he was working with you to try and find out who killed his Grandma, and that you needed that address book that Benjy found. When we leave here we are going to find him, that dirty bugger, and beat the truth out of him. Nobody puts our Rev in the soup and gets away with it. And you can't stop us!" As he spoke the last words he was shouting.

"I know I can't stop you, but I would like to try. First off, you both know that Stan would never want you to resort to violence for him. That's not what his religion is all about. But if you don't care that he doesn't want you to do it, and plan to go ahead anyway, think about this. If you clobber the guy that found the book, you may scare away the guys he got the book from, and we may never find them. If we don't find that book, we may never figure out who killed Mrs. Toskini. We've lost it twice; maybe the third time will be a charm. I think Stan would be pretty unhappy if you messed things up."

"I have to admit you have made some pretty good points, but it is hard to let this thing go. Someone needs to pay for it. Rev saved a lot of us from pretty rotten lives. We don't take it kindly when they hurt him. We will wait a while and see what you can do. But if something don't happen pretty quick, we will be right back into it." Toby looked at Rocks for confirmation. They both stood up at the same time and Arlen decided that everyone associated with Stan was super-sized.

"That's fair enough. I might could use some help on this thing. Can I get in touch with you guys if I need you?"

"Sure!" Rocks reached into his pocket and pulled out a little wallet full of business cards. Here's our card. Just give us a call. We always carry our cell phones."

As the men lumbered out the doorway Arlen chuckled and thought, *even the motorcycle gangs are businessmen nowadays.*

He hadn't even gotten the door closed all the way when he heard a soft knock. He swung the door open and was surprised to find Mia standing there.

"Mr. Arlen, the desk clerk told me about those men. They looked pretty tough. Are you all right?"

"I don't guess they're any more dangerous than your Mr. Devon, and at least these guys are my friends. I am fine. Goodnight."

She didn't smile as she turned away and he locked the door for the night.

CHAPTER 10

A rlen was up and had already returned from breakfast when Lt. Crowder began to beat dents into his door.

"How would you like to go over to see Toskini this morning?"

"Sure, I'm as ready as I'll ever be. I would like to find out where Stan got that address book and if he had another chance to look at it."

Lt. Crowder led the way down the hall and Arlen followed as fast as he was able, pushing his walker in front of him. He waited outside the door while Crowder went and got his car. He was surprised when, instead of a black and white, he drove up in a big blue SUV. He came around and opened the passenger door wide.

"Need some help?" He moved aside and held out his big hand.

"Nah, I think I can make it." Arlen still hated to admit that he needed help.

After he had struggled for a minute trying to get his feet up on the high running board, the lieutenant gripped his elbow firmly and propelled him up into the wide front seat.

"Thanks. I have a little trouble asking for help. I guess I'll have to be humble someday," he said, as Lt. Crowder headed around to the driver's side.

As he settled in behind the wheel, the lieutenant said, "I wouldn't be afraid to ask for a little help now and again. Might make your life a little easier, and besides most of us like to help if we know how." He fastened his seat belt and drove off looking a little embarrassed.

Arlen thought, *well, the tough police guy has a heart, too!* It seemed out of character, but it worked for him.

Arlen found one of the advantages of being a police officer when they got to the hospital. The lieutenant pulled a little plaque out of the glove drawer under the seat and put it in the window and pulled into a reserved police parking place just outside of the emergency entrance. He ran around and opened the door, and this time Arlen let him help him down from the high seat.

Lt. Crowder handed him his walker and headed off at a swift pace through the emergency entrance. Arlen followed as he wended his way through several hallways and ended up somehow at the front desk. A volunteer in a pinkish jacket was sitting there doing a crossword puzzle. As the lieutenant approached she looked up and smiled.

"Can I help you sir?"

"What room is Stan Toskini in?"

"Just a minute and I'll look it up." She pulled a sheaf of papers out of a drawer and scanned them. "I'm sorry sir, we don't show a Mr. Toskini in any room. Could he be someplace else?"

"How about ICU?" The lieutenant looked impatient. The volunteer picked up the phone, dialed a number and spoke quietly into it for a minute and hung it up. "Sorry, sir, I have no information about anyone by that name." She looked back down at her puzzle.

Crowder smiled and motioned to Arlen and walked off down to the end of the lobby.

"You know where he is, so why did you ask her?"

"Unless the sick person says they want people to know they are in the hospital, she is supposed to not know anything. She passed the test. Stan was in no shape to sign a permission paper when he came in, and under the HIPPA law he has to do that or officially he's not here. Keeps sick people from being bothered, which is a good thing, except that sometimes even the family can't find out if a loved one is in the hospital." He stopped and waited for Arlen to rest for a minute.

"Do you always act like a cop?"

The lieutenant smiled, but didn't answer.

Then they headed down a quiet hallway, past the chapel and past the gift shop, past offices and the hospital library, into the guts of the building, finally coming to two big wooden doors. Over the doors they saw a big sign that said 'Intensive Care Unit, Please Ring the Bell'. Beside the door was a dirty gray box sticking out of the wall. In the middle of the box was a big red button, which the lieutenant pushed vigorously. When nobody came for a minute he jammed his thumb on it again. Arlen saw that he was another guy who didn't like to wait.

A smallish woman in green scrubs pushed one of the doors open and said, "May I help you?"

Lt. Crowder pulled out his badge folio and put it near her face. "We are here to see Stan Toskini. Police business."

"Wait until I get the doctor. I can't let you in without the doctor's approval." With that she slammed the door shut, and Arlen could see the red creeping up Crowder's neck.

Almost before he could say anything the door swung open again, and a tall thin man with a black stethoscope hanging around his neck stuck his head out and smiled at them. "Sorry about that, but we are trying to be security minded these days. Come on in. How are you, Lieutenant?"

"I'm fine, Doc, we need to see Mr. Toskini. How is he doing?"

"Well, you know, he is recovering mighty fast. We are moving him out of here today into a regular room, so if you want to talk to him, you had better do it before they come to take him away." He held the door open wide and they walked in.

"Doc, this is Mr. Arlen. He and Toskini were working together on a problem at his assisted living facility. He needs to be here as well."

The doctor stuck out his hand, and as Arlen grabbed it he was surprised at the strength of the doctor's grip.

"Hi, Mr. Arlen. Mr. Toskini's in 3. It's right over there." He pointed to a small cubicle open at the front and full of medical instruments. "Now you'll have to excuse me, we've got quite a load today. Nice to meet you, Mr. Arlen." He spun round and headed toward another cubicle.

As they walked into the room, Stan saw them and smiled and then winced.

"It only hurts when I smile, to quote an old adage," he said.

"How are you doing, Stan," Arlen asked, surveying the purple and blue bruises covering his face and arms.

"Oh, I'm doing fine. Still just a little weak. I hope to get out of this place as soon as possible. My HMO gets mad at me when I spend their money."

"Do you feel like talking, Mr. Toskini?" Crowder asked, stepping up to the side of the bed. He was very careful not to touch or move any of the several tubes and wires that were strung from a maze of electronic boxes to various parts of Toskini's anatomy. Arlen saw that the lieutenant had obviously been in an intensive care unit before.

"Sure, but I'm pretty mystified myself. Whoever is doing these things isn't some amateur. They have access to lots of sources of information. My motorcycle friends are really discreet about their doings, but somehow someone found out that Benjy had the book and were able to trace him back to me. Have you found Benjy, Lieutenant?"

"No, but we are still looking. I have to say we don't get much cooperation from the motorcycle guys. They have an instinctive dislike for the police, but we are really trying."

"I can help on that when I get out of here. They might listen to me. Benjy is a good man, I pray he isn't in trouble because of me."

"Maybe when he heard of what happened to you he just dropped out of sight for a while. He may show up at any time." Crowder's expressionless face wasn't very encouraging in spite of his positive words.

Arlen broke in "Stan, how in the world did he find the book? Where was it?"

"That's the weird part, Arlen. I don't know. Benjy just came in the other evening and said 'is this what you are looking for?' and left. He hadn't been gone ten minutes when my door was broken down, and these two goons came in and started working me over and asking where the book was. Then one of them spotted it on the dining-room table, and they picked it up and left. It was a good thing for me that they did see it. They were really good at what they were doing. I don't think I would be alive today if they had finished the job. The Lord was looking out for me even though I don't deserve it."

"That means we are back at square one," Arlen moaned, feeling a little sorry for himself. He snapped right out of it when he took another look at Stan. He thought, *he is the one who got hurt trying to be my legs*, and he was ashamed of himself once more.

They said their good-byes and the lieutenant drove back to Meadowview, not saying much. He left Arlen at the door and drove off.

When he got to his room and lay down on his bed, he suddenly realized how much the trip had taken out of him and how much energy he had used up. He remembered how the detective in some of his favorite stories never left his home, but still solved great mysteries by using his vast deductive powers. He finally went to sleep thinking about how impossible that really sounded.

When he woke up in the morning he was still without a clue. In fact, he seemed to be even more confused, and he was also a little disappointed. He had been hoping that Stan had gotten some information that would help them break open the logjam, but all he had ended up with was pain and bruises. Not only that, but the book was gone again, this time probably for good. They wouldn't make the same mistake twice. In addition to that, Stan was apparently out of service for a while, so he had lost his legs. The only bright spot was that he saw Lt. Crowder as a little more human after their trip.

A very light tap on his door startled him and he hollered, "just a minute, I'm still in bed. He swung his walker over beside the bed and pulled himself up. He threw his robe over his shoulders and shuffled over to the door.

"Sorry to bother you so early, Mr. Arlen, but this package had a rush delivery label on it so I figured you would want it as soon as possible." The messenger held out a little rectangular box.

Arlen took the box and looked at the address label. What in the world was George doing now? "Thanks for the delivery. I don't know what my nephew is sending me but it must be important."

After the deliverer had gone, he shuffled over to his desk and set the box down and slid into the chair. He got out his little slicer and cut the tape from the box ends and opened it. There was a letter folded up in the top, and under that a box containing a cell phone. He picked up the letter and started to read.

Dear Unc.

Since you seem to be in the habit of being locked in small spaces, I thought you might need this. I have started your service with this company. The phone is easy to use and has big numbers on it so you can see it. Arlen snorted, "That's right, we old men can't see." The letter continued. Take a few minutes to learn how to use it. It might help you some day. You can set the speed dial for 911 and everything. Call me on it to let me know you got it. Here is your new phone number...

Love, George

Arlen almost threw the phone against the wall, but suddenly it began to play music. He didn't know how to stop it, so he put it back in the box and closed the lid. His regular phone suddenly began to ring so he got up and shuffled over to his bedside table and picked it up. "Arlen here."

"Hi, Unc. Did you get it? I tried calling you on it but you didn't answer. How do you like it? It's a good one, just made for you older folks. It's even got a camera in it..."

"Stop talking for a minute so I can get a word in edgewise. Why did you send me this thing? I've got a perfectly good phone right here on my table. Besides, it didn't ring. The dumb thing just started playing music."

"That was your ring tone. Nobody's phone sounds like the old land lines. When you hear music just push the little green picture of a phone and start talking. I'm gonna hang up and call you on it. Pick it up this time. Bye."

"Wait a minute!" The cell phone began playing music inside of the box. He fumbled it open and pushed the green button and said, "Arlen here."

"Hi, Unc. See how great it works? Have you gotten in any more trouble? Do you need me to come back out?"

"Thanks for the phone, George, but I wish you would quit worrying about me, I am fine. Did they fire you for coming out here?"

"No, no, I found out that this company has all sorts of perks for employees. They called what I did 'compassionate leave.' No prob."

"I'm glad things worked out for you, but please quit worrying about me. You will upset Beth and the kids. They don't need to know all about their old infirm relative. Give my love to all of them. Goodbye."

"I didn't mean to bother you, Uncle Arlen, I just worry about you, with us being so far away. I'm glad you're okay. I'll be talking to you soon."

"Thanks a lot, George. I'm sorry I'm so crabby. I appreciate the love you are showing for me and how much you care. It means a whole lot to me. I'll talk to you soon."

***

As soon as he was transferred to a regular room, Stan started trying to get himself checked out of the hospital. He knew that there were hospital discharge planners, doctors and other officials who wanted to know what is going to happen to you when you leave their care. They all have to sign off before you can walk, or be wheeled out of the facility.

Finally he got tired of waiting and called one of his friends, "Hey, Toby can you get a wheelchair and bring it over to my hospital room"

"Sure, Rev, be over in about ten minutes."

Stan was up sitting on the edge of his bed when Toby rolled a wheelchair through the open door of the room.

"Here it is. Whatcha gonna do with it."

"Help me get in and I'll show you."

Toby locked the wheels of the chair and grabbed Stan's arm and helped him into the seat. "What now."

"Wheel me down to your truck and take me home."

"Can we do that?"

"I don't know, let's try."

He had barely been pushed into his own front door when the phone started bouncing up and down on the table. He answered it and a loud strident voice yelled in his ear, "You can't just walk out of this hospital, Sir. You haven't been checked out properly. You must come back immediately."

"I'd like to, but I don't have the strength. How about you getting the papers ready, and I'll have someone bring me down in the morning to sign them. I am through being in the hospital."

"Well sir," the loud voice exclaimed, "If you are unable to come back today we will send an ambulance out to pick you up."

"NO! Don't do that. I told you I would be back in the morning. Some of my friends might get upset if you tried to force me back today. I don't want to be the cause of any trouble."

There was a long silence. Then, "Are your friends those motorcycle men that were in your room all the time?"

"Yes, I'm sorry, but they are pretty territorial. They seem to want to protect me."

"I see. I guess it will be fine if you can come in tomorrow morning, but remember, the hospital will *not* take *any* responsibility for the time that you left our care until you are back here. Is that understood?"

"Yes sir, and thanks for your patience." Stan chuckled and hung up the phone.

CHAPTER 11

Arlen had been brought up by parents who were moral people. Not religious, but moral. He remembered when he was a kid, and one day he found a dollar lying in the driveway. He had learned later that his cousin Johnny had dropped it when his folks came to pick him up after he had been visiting them. Arlen's big mistake had been to grab it up and quickly stuff it into his pocket instead of trying to find out who it belonged to. His dad always seemed to know when he was trying to get away with something, and this was no exception. He finally had to give Johnny back the dollar bill and one of his own as well.

But his newspaper work had made him pretty skeptical of Christians and their type of morality. Grandma, his dad's mother, was the only one in his family that he knew who even went to church. She had told him many times that she was praying for him.

Anyway, that was how he had grown up. Other people's stuff belonged to them and his stuff belonged to him. He guessed that was what made him so mad about the Meadowview property swindle. He was going to find out how it was all connected to Mrs. Toskini's death if he had to die trying. *Oops*, he thought, *he was pretty sure that could be arranged.*

As he thought about it, he decided he would really like to meet the guy who lived on the other side of him. So far he didn't think he had ever seen him, at least not to know who it was. He wasn't sure if it was by choice, but not only had he not seen him at meals, he didn't think he had seen him in the TV room, the lobby or any place else that the inmates gathered.

Well, he had barged in on his other neighbor and found her dead, maybe he would have better luck with this guy, but whatever happened he was going to meet him. No one had moved into Mrs. Toskini's room and he liked to know his neighbors. He wished he was able to move around better, but he decided he really should take Stan's advice and be thankful for what he had. At least he could still move around.

So he sat up and pulled his walker toward him and headed for the door. Down the hall he stopped in front of an identical door. Neither he nor his neighbor had put any decorations on their doors as many of the others had, so they were pretty bare. Surprisingly, there wasn't even a nametag on this door. After he got there, he became a little more reluctant. Then he thought, *hey, he's just another inmate of this place. What could happen?* For an instant he thought of a lot of things that could happen, but he banged on the door with his walker. Then he banged again. Not a sound escaped from behind the wheelchair-wide door. As he turned to head back to his room, he saw a youngish, very muscular man rushing down the hall from the elevators. When he got close to Arlen, his dark face wrinkled into a grimace.

"What you want?" he growled.

"Hi, my name is Arlen, I just wanted to meet my next-door neighbor." He tried to send a smile back against the frown.

"Why you want to do that? I don't want to meet you!" He shuffled to one side trying to get around Arlen

"Well, 's'cuse me." Now Arlen's face matched his neighbor's. He turned his walker and started back toward his own door. The other man fumbled a shiny set of keys out of his pocket and shoved one in the lock. Suddenly a black book slipped out from among the papers he had under his arm and plopped on the floor. He squatted faster than Arlen thought a man his size could move and grabbed it up and disappeared into his room.

Arlen closed his door in a daze. He would bet his walker against a used Kleenex that it was the missing address book he had seen. Now he had something else to chew on while he tried to go to sleep.

He remembered how easy it had been to go to sleep when he was a kid. Except maybe for Christmas Eve or the night before his birthday. He was thinking about the regular days when he used to fall asleep in the back seat of their car and how his dad had to carry him into his bunk bed. Or to the times when his mom would come into his bedroom and start to read a book to him and never got past page five before he was sound asleep.

That had all changed with age. In the first place he often had trouble getting to sleep, and by three AM the pain would wake him up, and he would have to take a pill to help him go to sleep again. That problem had been helped some by his new medication, but now with mysteries and murders to ponder, he was having more and more trouble sleeping. The result was that he was constantly run down. And now he was pretty scared, as well.

The guy next door knew that he knew he had the address book. *Not only that,* he thought, *he knows how to get into my room. It must have been him that took the book the night he heard the noise. If he is the one who really murdered Mrs. Toskini, I am going to have to be much more careful.*

The clang of the phone always startled Arlen, and this time was no exception.

"Arlen here."

"Hi, Arlen, it's Stan Toskini. How's it going?"

"Hey, Stan, how are you feeling? Shouldn't you be resting?"

"That's all my guys will let me do here, I'm getting pretty tired of lying around. I've had some time to think about

Gram's death. It must have something to do with them trying
to force you to give them your property. Why else would Mia
be so adamant that Gram wasn't murdered."

"Why indeed. And here's one that will curdle your milk.
I think the guy who lives next door to me has your address
book. He dropped it while he was snubbing me out in the hall
a little while ago. What do you think about that?"

"Say, brother, you had better be careful. That guy must
know how to get into your room. You need to figure out how
to block the door with a chair or something."

"Hadn't thought of that, but it is a good idea. I'll jam my
guest chair against the doorknob. I'm a little worried about
Devon too. They may be working together. They're a pretty
rough pair. I feel sort of hemmed in here."

"Well, I'll be back on my feet in a couple of days. In the
meantime you had better talk to Lt. Crowder again. He might
be willing to look after you a bit. Gotta go now, I see Rocks
frowning at me. See ya soon."

Arlen would like to call Crowder again, but the lieutenant
didn't seem too excited about him or his problems. He figured that he was just a burr under the officer's saddle and that
he would prefer not to hear from him. He had just finished
pondering these thoughts and pulling himself up to the desk
when the phone jangled again.

He shuffled back to his bed and said, "Arlen here."

"Mr. Arlen, this is Lt. Crowder. I hear that you think you
have found the address book again. I'm pretty interested
in that."

"How the heck did you hear that? Is my room bugged too?"
Arlen heard a low chuckle from the phone.

"No, Mr. Toskini called. He's worried about you and said
he couldn't get out to help you. I wish you'd both just leave
things to us. We are working on it."

"I'm sure you are, Lieutenant, and right now I wish I was
out of it. I don't feel very sanguine about the future of my

health with this big guy next door. He knows how to get into my room, you know."

"It appears so, or at least he knows someone who knows how to get into your room. You'd best block your door at night until we get this sorted out. I don't want to come over there and find that you've fallen out of bed too."

"Those are the nicest words you have ever said to me, Lieutenant. Does this mean that you now believe Mrs. Toskini was murdered?" Arlen smiled to himself.

"It sure is beginning to look like it. But as I told you before, I'm keeping my options open. I just called to tell you to be careful. I'll look into this guy a little and be over tomorrow to check his place out. So be careful!"

He chuckled again and thought, *that lieutenant is getting downright human!*

It was funny what exhaustion could do. Arlen slept through the entire night without waking up once and it took him awhile in the morning to remember the menacing guy next door. It made him wonder if he really wanted to go down to breakfast. He had never been too hot on breakfast anyway. But he decided that he couldn't hide in his room for the rest of his life, so gathering his trusty walker and pulling the chair away from the door, he opened it and moved out into the hall.

As he closed and locked the door, he turned and saw his neighbor clumping down the hall toward the elevators. That left him with another choice. He could go on or he could go back to his room and wait for another elevator. Oh well, he thought, life is a mystery, and so he moved in behind his neighbor and followed him into the elevator. When the elevator doors closed, the man stood like a statue staring at the door and never even seemed to notice that Arlen was there. When they got to the lobby, the guy rushed out and down the hall before Arlen could even step out of the elevator.

Arlen breathed a sigh of relief and sat down and enjoyed his breakfast more than he thought he could enjoy food at that time of day. He decided, *maybe it is my mind telling me that it is good to be alive.*

After breakfast, he walked down the front hall and rang the little bell that sat on the counter. Mia came out of the adjoining office and smiled at him.

"Good Morning, Mr. Arlen. What can I do for you this beautiful morning?"

"You can tell me who my next door neighbor is and why he is so obnoxious," he answered shortly.

"Mr. Max Pender lives next door to you. He was the latest to move into your floor before you came. I don't know anything about him except that he keeps strictly to himself and doesn't talk to anyone. Perhaps if you got acquainted it would be good for both of you."

"I tried that and he just about bit my head off. Besides that, I believe that he has something that belonged to Mrs. Toskini, and I would like to get it back and give it to Stan. He had found it and someone came and beat the stuffing out of him and took it away from him."

He remembered his words to Stan about being a blabbermouth, because his words seemed to affect her deeply. She turned very pale, glanced around the lobby then turned back and said, "Mr. Arlen, go back to your room right now. I will be up there in five minutes. We have to talk."

Since he was headed back to his room anyway, he decided he would do what she told him. Besides, he was very interested in what she had to say.

He had barely closed the door to his room when there was a knock, and before he had time to say "come in" she was inside and closing the door. She marched to the vase someone had put on his desk and pulled the flowers out. She shook them and looked under the vase. Then she pulled the big picture away from the wall and looked behind it. He sat on his bed in amazement. What in the world was she looking for? After looking under the table and in his bathroom, she turned on his new TV and turned up the volume and came and sat down on the bed beside him, almost tipping him over. "Mr. Arlen, you and Mr. Toskini are in this thing way over your heads. I am going to tell you some things so that you will realize what a dangerous game you are playing. And, believe me, it's not really a game, it's deadly."

"Are you threatening me?" He realized how dumb it was the minute he had said it, but it was the best thing his overloaded brain could come up with. He suddenly realized that she had been searching for bugs like those that had been in Mrs. Toskini's room.

CHAPTER 12

"M r. Arlen, I am an undercover INS agent. I was sent here to replace the agent who was investigating this case previously. So far no one knows I am an agent, and I have to keep it that way, or I may end up in the same lake where they found Hector. You are really making things difficult for me by stirring the pot."

"Now look, Mia, or whatever your name really is, why should I believe that story? Do you have any credentials? Of course not. I do know my friend couldn't find any trace of you on the Internet, so I know you aren't Mia Carson. But how do I know that you aren't part of the people who are doing whatever it is that they are doing?" He still didn't sound very coherent.

"Mr. Arlen, let me give you a little history lesson. From the time that President Reagan said, 'Mr. Khrushchev, tear down this wall' through the implosion of the former Soviet Union, the old communist movers and shakers have been jockeying for their own individual powers. The former security chiefs and their agents had already been building their own private power organizations, filling in voids left by the crumbling government structure. Most of these enterprises operated in shady areas or were downright illegal.

As time passed, the more active groups in each country joined forces, either peacefully or violently, and eventually a well-organized Mafia type organization blanketed the countries that had made up the old Soviet Union, and gradually spread out over the world. Implanted agents in many countries joined the mélange, merely exchanging one system for another, sometimes even with the same bosses. They have been in operation for years now. It's one of these organizations we are dealing with. They are huge and ruthless and hard to stop. That's why we can't let anyone set us back at this stage of the game. Do you understand?"

"I think so. At least it sounds reasonable right now." Arlen leaned back, even more confused.

"Who do you think let you out of the record room? I nearly blew my cover that time, but I couldn't let you die down there. I couldn't come in and help you either, because someone might have been watching. I was very glad to see you coming out of that freight elevator, but I couldn't tell you so."

"Who are these particular people?"

"Just leave it at the fact that they aren't exactly friendly. It's a good thing I happened to glance at the surveillance screen while you were still in the hall, but I didn't see who locked you in. Since we don't record that data, I couldn't find out. But leave Mr. Pender strictly alone. I have been investigating him, but haven't found out much. It is quite possible that he is one of them." She lay her hand lightly on his arm. "Please be careful."

"Well, he sure is an obnoxious cuss anyway. Besides that, I think he knows how to get into my room. He stole the book from me the other night."

"I've got to go. I can't spend too much time here, or it will look suspicious." She got up from the bed.

"It was Mrs. Toskini's address book that I was telling you about down below. Stan and I found it hidden in her room. Pender has it now."

"How do you know that?" She turned back to him.

"He dropped it when he was trying to avoid me the other night. He picked it up so fast it was pretty obvious he knew that I saw it." He wondered why he suddenly trusted her with all of that information. After all, she may or may not be who she said she was.

"I will try and watch Mr. Pender more closely, but you had better be more careful. I will have your lock changed, but he may still be able to get in. Our locks are not very secure. Put something in front of your door before you go to sleep. If you think someone is trying to get in, press your button and I will have someone up here as fast as I can. I don't want you to end up like Mrs. Toskini. Now I'm leaving." She pulled open the door and stuck her head out and then followed it with the rest of her body without saying another thing.

As he lay back on his bed, pushing the button to get more support on his back, it suddenly came to him. She said, 'like Mrs. Toskini.' She had known all along that it was murder. He began to realize why she tried so hard to keep him from snooping into it. She didn't want things stirred up, but that's exactly what he had done.

His phone jangled. He grabbed it and said, "Arlen here."

"Hi, Arlen, it's me, Stan. You awake?"

"I am now. What's up?"

"Your Mia doesn't exist. She must be using a phony name. My guy just spent hours checking her out. I would be very cautious around her."

"Yeah, I'm way ahead of you this time. Mia told me who she is. I can't tell you any more over the phone, but I'll bring you up to speed the next time you can get over here." He thought, *there goes my big mouth again. I've got to be careful about her identity. It might get her killed.* "But I need you to look up another person, Max Pender. He is my next-door neighbor, the one who dropped your grandma's address book. He doesn't seem like a very friendly fellow, and I'd really like to know who he is and why such a young man is in an assisted living facility."

"I'll get my guy right on it. I hope you are putting something in front of your door at night so you don't have any more visitors."

"It's funny, you told me that before and then Lt. Crowder suggested it and now Mia even recommended that I do the same thing! It is making me paranoid, so I am following all your advice. And remember, she isn't what she seems." He was surprised to realize that he really did believe her story and was glad she was on their side.

"Well, I don't know if that's good or bad, but I guess you will tell me soon enough. I'll get back to you on Pender."

Arlen decided he would make a list of what he knew like some of the famous fictional detectives did. He was utterly confused and he thought he needed some kind of order.

Mrs. Toskini was obviously murdered.

Lt. Crowder is beginning to believe it.

Mia's predecessor was also murdered.

Mrs. Toskini's address book was important – everybody wants it and Stan has been beaten up for it.

Pender has the notebook, but who is Pender?

Mia is an INS agent, if I believe her.

Mia saved my life, if I believe her.

I believe her.

So someone else had tried to kill me.

Meadowview has a racket of taking guest's property from them.

Don't know if the INS and the property scam are tied together.

Boy, that's not much to go on, he thought and wondered if his little gray cells were up to it. Then he shuddered; realizing it wasn't just a fun fictional story, but a real, live, deadly problem.

CHAPTER 13

M ax Pender. *I sure can't get used to that name.* He couldn't use the name that his parents had blessed him with in Dushanbe, that was certain. *Firuz Sarhad, now that is a fine name,* he thought. He wished he could use it, but if he did he would be sent back to Tajikistan, and if he went back to Tajikistan he wouldn't have any name at all. Now he was in a terrible mess. *That guy next door knows I have the notebook. If he talks to the police I will be deported.* He wished the men would come and pick up that address book. He didn't want to be responsible for it any more. They just wanted to get him in trouble again.

Ever since he had left Tajikistan things had gone from bad to worse. First getting the phony papers to get into this country. That had cost his wife a lot. Then those guys black-mailing him into helping them. Then that poor lady dying. *Even though I didn't do it, I knew what had been going on,* he thought. Now they were going to want him to help them do something to that Arlen man. He just didn't think he could take it anymore. He had tried to scare him off by locking him in the basement, but that didn't help. He didn't know who had let him out of the record room, but he was glad that he had gotten out and hadn't died, too. *But,* he thought, *that Arlen isn't the kind of guy to scare easily.* They were probably going to have to do something much more severe and he hated it.

A loud rap on the door interrupted his thoughts.

"Yes?"

"Open the door!"

"Go away!"

"Open the door or we'll break it down!" The pounding got more insistent.

"OK, OK, a minute."

He cautiously opened the door a crack. It was jammed back in his face, and two very large men shoved him roughly aside and rushed into the room.

"What you want?"

"Shut up Pender. We came for the notebook, and you are going with us. Get your coat!"

"I'm not going with you. Here is the notebook, you don't need me."

"We don't, but the boss wants to see you. Don't think we won't carry you out if we need to. There is a very nice wheelchair out in the hall. Be a good boy so we don't have to hurt anyone."

They went out of the room single file. One walked in front of him and the other walked closely behind him, poking something very hard in his back. As they passed the lobby the night receptionist said, "Hello. Are you going out?"

The man in front said, "He's going for a ride with us."

The lady smiled and said, "Oh, that's nice. Have a good ride, Mr. Pender." Pender didn't say anything because he felt the hard thing poking in his back, and he couldn't let the nice lady get hurt.

A small blue sedan was parked out in a visitor's space. The motor was running, and behind the wheel sat a very small man with a hawk-like face. His sharp nose was so hooked it almost met his chin. They shoved Pender in the back seat, and the car took off, peeling rubber in the parking lot.

Nobody spoke as the little man pushed the car through the light evening traffic. Max was really worried that they didn't care if he saw where they were going. Perhaps they didn't expect to bring him back. He was sure that the two guys who had come into his room were the same two he had seen when he had picked up his forged papers at Vahdat Palace in Dushanbe. They had been hanging around the office where he had been sent to get them.

They stopped in front of an old suburban house, and the one with the gun, or whatever he kept poking Max with, did it again, and motioned toward the door of the house. They marched up the sidewalk with the hawk-faced man leading the way. He rapped loudly on the door. It was opened a crack and then was pulled wide open, and they followed the man inside.

The house obviously wasn't really lived in. They went into what must have once been the living room, where there were three or four white plastic chairs and a scarred card table spread out in the middle of the floor. There was no other furniture in the room and no pictures on the walls. The card table was lighted by an overhead light in the ceiling. A tall, dark-skinned man in a grimy gray sweatshirt sat in one of the chairs behind the table.

"Well, did he give you the notebook?"

"Sure, boss, he knows what's good for him. What do you want us to do with him now?"

"Kill him!"

"Uh, boss," the other man said, "that dame at Meadowview saw us go out with him. She may remember that if he shows up dead."

The tall dark man shoved the table away and jumped up. "You dopes! How did that happen? I told you to be careful! Now we'll have to think of something else. Lock him in the bedroom until we can figure it out. Androv, you keep guard on the door."

He was pushed and shoved down a dark back hallway and into a carpeted room and thrown on the floor. The door slammed shut. There was no furniture in the room. It must have been the master bedroom because he noticed a door opening into a bathroom at one side. As he sat on the floor, he thought about his cell back in Tajikistan. After the collapse of the Soviet Union his country was in a terrible mess for a very long time. He didn't know where all the gangs had come from, but he knew that everyone was afraid of them. When his boss at the aluminum factory had asked him to cheat on some invoices, he was scared not to. Then the police had found out and he had been arrested. The police were worse than the gangs. They demanded a lot of money to let him out and when he said he didn't have it, they beat him every day for two weeks and then left him in his tiny cell to rot.

Finally some men had gone to his wife, Anna, and said they would get him out for 1000 Euros. Somehow his Anna had come up with the money. He didn't know how and had been afraid to ask, but they had given him some phony parole papers and had gotten him released. He still owed them for the steamer trip to America and for the plane ride to the West Coast. And Anna hadn't come. He was trying to pay them back, but it was very slow, and they were blackmailing him so he would owe them money for the rest of his life, and he would never be able to bring Anna to America. She was better off in their homeland. Otherwise she might be sitting on the floor with him. He knew that he would never see her again. They had been married six years and they had hoped soon to afford to be able to have one son. But if those guys hadn't gotten him out he would still be in that tiny cell or dead.

He had been on the floor for a couple of hours and it was beginning to feel pretty hard. The door lock rattled and the door swung open. The hawk-faced man came in balancing a plate and a glass. He could see a big man standing directly in the doorway. He had a gun in his belt that Max hadn't noticed before.

The hawk-faced man put the plate and the glass on the floor and whispered softly, "Watch yourself, I will try and help you later," and backed out the door.

Max thought, *well, that's very odd. I have a friend in this house*. He couldn't see how the man could help him, but at least now he had a glimmer of hope.

As he sat back on the floor, eating, he came to a decision. Even if they let him go, he wasn't going to help them kill that Arlen. They could send him back to prison, but he wasn't going to be involved in another murder. If he got out, God willing, he would try to figure out some way to help break down their organization and stop them from using more poor people to make money. And he would get his Anna over here. With that thought his tired body fell into a troubled sleep.

He was suddenly wide-awake as the door lock began rattling. The door opened a crack and a hand slipped in and suddenly the light was off, and it was pitch black.

"Shh. It's me. I'm going to get you out of here, but you have to trust me. If they find us they will kill us." The little man was framed in the dim light of the doorway.

Max decided right away that he would trust him. He couldn't be in any worse shape than he was in already. So he quickly followed the man out the door. The man closed it and locked it again, then grabbed Max's arm and pulled him down the hall. Suddenly they heard a deep Russian speaking voice coming from the other end of the hall. The man grabbed Max and pulled him through an open door and closed it very quietly. The voice faded away as whoever it was headed toward the back of the house. The man opened the door and almost dragged him back out into the dark hallway. He pulled him toward the front of the house, quietly opened the front door, pushed him out on the porch, and silently swung the door closed behind him. Pender ran down the street, almost on tiptoe, trying not to make any noise. There was no traffic and the lights were out in all the houses on the block. He looked at his watch and saw it was almost two o'clock in the morning. *Now what?* He pondered. *I don't have any idea of where to go.* If he went back to Meadowview, they would just come and get him again. If he went to the police, he would most likely be deported. He hoped the bad men wouldn't find out that it was the little man who had let him go.

The area he was in looked pretty dingy and run down. He thought, *even here, a few blocks makes quite a difference in the character of the city.* He entered an area with pawnshops and small stores, and then he saw a store that he didn't quite understand. It was some kind of a church. There was a cross, painted on the big plate-glass window, and a bunch of motorcycles were parked in a neat row out in front. The lights inside sent their fluorescent beams out, causing the brightly painted bikes to glow in the dark street.

He could see through the window that there were twelve or fifteen men inside. They were all dressed in black leather pants and dark shirts or completely done up in faded blue denim. Many of them had jackets with big designs on the back. He couldn't tell what the designs meant from outside, but he remembered seeing similar emblems on those men they called Hell's Angels, and he knew that they were supposed to be bad people. The man in charge looked as tough as the rest. He was sitting on a high stool in the front of the group, and his hair was pulled back in a knot at the nape of his neck. The man swung his arms as he was talking, and Max noticed the unusual tattoos on his arms. They were the strangest designs he had ever seen, big bright colored patterns like an abstract painting.

As he stood wondering what to do, his mind drifted to the old country again, and the Orthodox Church he and Anna had attended. He had loved the cool, quiet sanctuary and the chanting of the priests and the formality of the service. This place wasn't like any of them, but maybe he could at least get some help from the leader man. If nothing else, maybe they could hide him for a while like his church had done.

His reverie was broken by a voice which said, "Come on in, brother. Come in. You are welcome here." As he had been dreaming, the big tattooed man had come to the door and was calling to him.

"I don't speak English too good."

"That's all right, come on in. I'm Stan Toskini." He put out a tattooed arm and pulled him into the room. Max felt like turning and running, but the pastor had a firm grip on his shoulder, so he let himself be lowered into a chair. He thought to himself, *it's funny how easy it still is for me to think in Tajik and how hard it still is to speak English.* It was even harder since he had spent a year in France after getting out of Tajikistan, waiting for his final papers and for the ship that was to bring him here.

"Why you open so late at night?" He asked.

"Well, tonight we got started and just kept on keeping on." The tattooed man answered, smiling at him. "Sometimes it happens that way. We have a lot to ask the Lord for, or to be forgiven for." Several of the big men laughed loudly and one of them said, "Amen to that!"

Max thought, *he's saying they are talking right to God. I don't know if that can be,* but he whispered, "I don't like interrupting, but we might talk?"

"Sure, what's on your mind?" Toskini plopped down in a chair beside him.

Max looked at him in fright. "Oh no, maybe all alone when you through here."

"No problem, just sit around and we'll have a talk when we get done. Grab yourself a cup of coffee."

Stan got up and moved back to the podium and sat on the high stool. He picked up a worn black Bible that looked ready to fall apart. It was stuffed with papers and notes that threatened to fly away as he waved the book. "Look guys, as I was saying, some of you have only heard Jesus' name as a swear word. Have you ever wondered about that? Why wouldn't people use some important name when they want to make a really powerful point? Why not John Kennedy, or Einstein or maybe even John Wayne. Those are powerful names everyone knows. They were, or are, big shots, important people. So why Jesus? It's easy. In spite of their unbelief, they know in their hearts that Jesus is the most powerful name in the universe, and in their ignorance they think they can invoke His name on their enemies. But you know that's not the way it works. Jesus isn't at anyone's beck and call. Some of you may think your gang buddies will always be with you, but deep in your hearts, you know that's not true. They die or they are tossed in jail, or worse, someone says you are making time with his girl and then who's your buddy? But Jesus isn't like that. He is available and you can call on him anytime, not as a curse, but to lift you out of the depths of hate and despair and to help you find your way. Now I know some of you are sitting there with some good questions, so let's hear them." He paused and waved his hand at the group and put his Bible back on the stand.

It was over an hour later when he had fielded all of their questions and all of the motorcycles had roared off in clouds of blue smoke, cracking the silence of the early morning.

Toskini stood up and stretched and walked back and sat down beside Max. "If you have trouble with English I probably can get a translator who speaks your language. What language do you normally speak?" He smiled a tired smile as he said it, but he saw that it shot a wave of fear through Max, and he could see his hands shake.

"That's okay, my English is work. I just need place to stay for a while."

"We sure can handle that. You can come over to my place. I always have a little extra room. Are you out of money?"

The calm question startled him. "No! No, it isn't that. Someone is looking for me and I can't let them find me."

"Oh, are you having trouble with immigration?"

"What you mean? I didn't say such!"

"Take it easy, don't get nervous. I was just trying to figure out a way to help you." Stan put his hand on the other's shoulder, but quickly removed it when he felt the man   quiver.

"Thank you, but I don't need help. Just a place to stay until I can figure out things."

"We can do that for you Mr....say, you never told me your name."

"Pender, Max Pender."

Suddenly Pender jumped back in fright as the pastor's face lighted up and he said, "You don't happen to live at Meadowview, do you?"

Max jumped up, pushing Toskini aside, and ran outside and down the dark street. He didn't stop until he was sure no one was following him and then leaned against a brick building, trying to recover his breath. His desperate thought was, *here I am back on the street and nowhere to go. It's so hard when you can't trust anyone.* He realized he was lucky that he still had some money left in his wallet. He decided he would find a hotel or motel to stay in until he could think things out. He was terrified that they would still find him as he walked into the dim sunrise.

CHAPTER 14

S tan stood staring out the door at Max's rapidly retreating
back. *I wonder what ghosts are pursuing him. He sure was
scared.* Stan well remembered what it was like to be scared.
Before he got blood poisoning he thought he was invincible.
He remembered that he would try anything. He decided that he
had been fortunate to never get as far as to do anything really
fatal. Sure, he drank a lot, but he could never see messing up
his mind with drugs, as some of his riding buddies had done.
He remembered one of the guys who had been on something
powerful and had decided that he could ride his bike through
a brick wall. He couldn't.

He remembered riding his bike down Eleventh Avenue. He
was saying out loud, "Man, I'm sick. What's happening to me?"

His motorcycle veered across the road. *Oh, I'm going to
pass out.* "Help me, somebody!" he hollered, and then his bike
hit the curb and bounced back into the middle of the wide
street, and slid under a car that had squealed to a stop.

The car driver hollered, "It wasn't my fault, he slid into me."

Several people ran out into the street flagging down the
slowly moving vehicles. Soon the paramedics scooped him up
and roared away. His buddies he had been riding with faded
into the traffic and soon were soon out of sight.

"Where am I?" he whispered gazing around the room with
bleary eyes.

A nurse leaned over his bed and said, "You're awake, great. You are in the emergency room of Community Hospital. You have been very sick."

"What's the matter with me? Am I going to die?"

"You'll have to ask the doctor all those questions." The nurse said over her shoulder as she walked out of the cubicle.

He wandered in and out of consciousness all day and woke up petrified that he was going to die. The doctor's short visits didn't help.

"Am I going to die? What can I do? I don't want to die!"

"I'm sorry, young man," the doctor said. "You passed out because blood poisoning and excess alcohol shut down your system. Then you were badly bruised and contused when you hit that car. I can't give you a prognosis yet, you are still very ill."

Stan thought about it and then suddenly said, "Where's my bike?"

"What bike are you talking about?" the doctor said as he turned to leave.

"My motorcycle!"

"Oh, the police have it impounded, I suppose. They had us do blood tests and you didn't have any drugs in your system, so we assume it was mainly the blood poisoning that caused you to crash"

"I don't want to die!" Stan grabbed the doctor's arm and held him.

"Let go of me. We are doing the best we know how, but it will be up to the good Lord to decide if you can shake this illness off. You let yourself get into pretty poor physical condition."

Stan let the doctor go and turned his face to the wall. After a few minutes he heard a voice behind him say, "may I talk to you for a moment?"

"No, go away."

"But I can help you. You are frightened that you are going to die. I can ease your mind."

Stan whirled around and gazed at the rotund Hispanic man who was standing beside his bed smiling at him. "Who are you? How can *you* help me? I'm going to die. Can you keep me from dying?"

"No, but I can show you how to face your future whether you live or you die."

"Are you a priest sent here to give me last rights? I don't believe in that stuff."

The man smiled and said, "No, I'm not a priest, and I'm not here to give you last rights. I am the hospital chaplain. My name is Jose Ramos, and I would like to help you to come to grips with this situation you are in. Jesus Christ can give you all the help you need."

"I don't believe in that stuff. I already told you that."

"Oh, you will, you will. And you will be eternally glad you did."

Stan had spent more days in ICU and horrifying nights when he dreamed he had died and gone to hell. He finally was afraid to go to sleep and was groggy all day.

"Mr. Toskini."

"Who are you?"

"I am the hospital administrator. We are going to have to do something about the bills you are running up by being here. Do you have insurance, or any way to pay?"

"No, I never needed any dumb insurance before, and I don't have a lot of money. How much do I owe you?"

When the man told him, he almost wished he had died. "I'm sorry, Mr. Toskini, but you are going to have to make some arrangements for your debt, or we will have to discharge you. We can't afford to keep footing your bills."

After he left Stan laughed bitterly. *I guess they'll throw me out on the street, even though I still may die. What in the world will I do?*

That night he was moved from ICU to a regular room, but was told it would only be temporary unless he could make some sort of large initial payment. When he woke up Chaplain Ramos was sitting in a chair beside his bed with his dark head bowed in prayer.

"What are you doing here? I can't pay you either."

Chaplain Ramos head jerked up and he smiled, "You don't have to pay me. I receive all I need. What is the matter?"

When Stan had whined about the hospital administrator's visit, the chaplain laughed and said, "Wow, that's a pretty bad fix. I don't blame you for whining. But it is time for you to get some backbone and quit feeling sorry for yourself. Have patience. I am working on an arrangement to get you admitted as an indigent. Then most of your bills will be taken over by a charitable group that I work with. Just remember, God is good."

He had given Stan a Bible and the next day he tried to plow through the Old Testament, but when he got to Exodus he gave up. *What good will all this historical junk do me?'* He threw the Bible onto the roll around table just as the chaplain walked in.

The chaplain's smile lit up his whole face and he said, "Reading your Bible! That's great. How is it going?"

"I don't understand any of this stuff. Why do you want me to read all this old historical junk? What good can it possibly do?"

The chaplain's smile grew. "I see the problem. This book isn't like an ordinary book, where you start at page one and go on to the end. You need to start reading in the New Testament. I'm sorry I forgot to tell you that. The Old Testament is for later on."

"I thought you wanted me to read the Bible, what is this New Testament?"

"Here, let me show you." He picked up the Bible and turned to the book of John. Now try this for a while, and see if it doesn't make sense to you. Write down any questions you have, and we can discuss them. Then we can take a look at Romans, the best book in the Bible."

"They told me again that they were going to throw me out. Do you know of any place I can go?"

"Don't worry about that, I've got it all taken care of. Just spend your time reading your Bible."

"Yeah, but I don't have much money and my biker friends have deserted me. I'm in a bad spot."

"You are going to come and stay with Rosa and me. We have plenty of room, and it will be a good place for you to heal and learn. Besides, my Rosa is the best cook in the state."

A week later in a small house in a quiet neighborhood, Stan pushed away from the table and said, "Rosa, I never knew what really good food was until I came here! Thank you for putting up with me."

"We enjoy having your company. Jose and I get a little lonely since our children left home. So it is our pleasure."

Their home *was* a perfect place to study the Bible, and he learned to pray and ask God to help him live a better life. Rosa answered all his questions when Jose was gone. Then one evening Jose came home and said to him, "how would you like to go to school?"

"I'm not very smart. What kind of school would I go to?"

"I can get you a full scholarship to Pacific Coast Bible College if you would like to go. Rosa graduated from there."

"But how would I live and buy food and all that? I don't have a job or any money."

"I told you it is all covered. Your dorm fees are paid by the scholarship and our church has volunteered to pay for your food and other expenses. I even know where you can get a job. All you have to do is stay on the straight and narrow and study hard. Think you can do that?"

"I would really like to give it a try."

The time came to leave for college and Stan was almost in tears. "Jose, Rosa, I've never had anyone love me the way you two have. My mom died shortly after I was born, and my dad abandoned me when I was ten, so I've never had any family love like this. I hope I can repay you some day, but I know I can never repay your love for me. It is invaluable."

"Your payment to us will be to succeed and make us proud of you," Rosa said through her tears.

With some hard work and much prayer he had graduated and now the Ramos' were at his graduation.

Rosa ran up and enfolded him in a big hug. "You did well. We are so proud of you. Jesus is good."

Jose shook his hand and said, "Do you have any plans for the future? You have a good education. There are many things you could do."

"You know," Stan said, looking at the big garish tattoos on his arms, "I keep thinking about those motorcycle gangers that I used to ride with. They are lost and headed for hell. I have been praying hard about it, and I think I am going to try and start a ministry to them. I can start with the guys I know and spread out. I'd like to go to rest stops along the highway and reach those guys who are out on the road in their pointless travels. Do you think I can do that?"

"What a great idea. I'm sure there are Christians who will donate each month to your ministry, and you will be free to reach the bikers. We will pray for you and help you when we can."

As Stan's mind popped back to the present he thought about Arlen and Meadowview and his grandma. He still couldn't believe that Grandma Toskini was dead. She had been so proud of him when he had graduated. She was the only member of his family who had been a Christian, and he found out that she had always prayed for him, even when he was on the wrong trail. He sure hoped he and Arlen could find out what had happened to her.

CHAPTER 15

A s the phone began jangling at him, Arlen was glad again that Mia had gotten it moved to his bedside table. He reached over and grabbed it and said, "Arlen here."

"Arlen, its Stan. You couldn't guess what happened last night. Pender came into my church looking for help. He said someone was chasing him. He doesn't speak English very well. If I had to guess, I'd say he's from Eastern Europe somewhere, but I'm not sure. When I recognized his name he turned tail and ran. I've got some boys out looking for him, but so far, no soap. He got real spooked when I mentioned the INS. Do you have any idea who is after him?"

Arlen sat up in bed and scratched his head. "That makes this mess all the confuseder, if that's even a word. I am now leaning more and more toward believing Mia. I think I'll lay it on her and see what she says."

"Just remember, I told you to be careful who you trust. But you are closer to it than I am. Keep me informed. I'll let you know if my guys find anything."

Arlen couldn't figure it out. If Pender was running maybe someone else knew he had the book. Or maybe they took it from him and that's why he was running.

When he called Mia, she was reluctant to come to his room again, so she told him to meet her in the weight room at the end of the hall. He hadn't been there yet, so he figured it would be an adventure. He sat on his bed, waiting impatiently for the half-hour she had asked for to pass, and then pushed his walker toward the end of the hall. He could see that the weight room door was already open. As he got nearer he could hear the heavy thud thud thud of running feet. Pushing his way into the room, he had to smile. She was running on a treadmill, the banging of her footsteps echoing down the hall. It was a well-equipped room with three treadmills along the west wall and three stationary bikes near the windows. Two bench press setups dominated the middle of the floor and there were several machines he couldn't even recognize along the eastern wall.

Mia coasted to a stop and jumped off the machine. The next thing he noticed was that there were no chairs in the room. Mia understood and took both of his hands and eased him down on the platform of the machine she had been running on.

She smiled and said, "We have to stop meeting this way."

Well, well, he thought, *she has a sense of humor too.*

"You might well be interested in what I have to tell you, if indeed, you are an INS agent."

"Mr. Arlen, you really need to trust me. I am what I say I am. But please don't say it too loud or too often." The smile had faded and an intensely serious frown had replaced it.

"Look, Mia, if I didn't trust you, I wouldn't be here. But you have to admit this a strange situation we have found ourselves in."

"Granted, Mr. Arlen, now what do you want to tell me?"

"Please just call me Arlen, will you? I just got a call from Stan Toskini. He told me that Max Pender had come into his church in the middle of the night looking for help. When he told Stan his name, and Stan asked him if he was from Meadowview, he took off like a scared rabbit. Stan has his minions out looking for him, but so far, no luck."

"I know he hasn't been back to his room. I also know that two big guys paid him a visit last night and he went out with them. He didn't say anything, but one of the guys told Shirley that he was taking a ride with them. He never came back."

"Let's go take a look into his room." Arlen struggled to get up.

"I can't do that. We have to respect everyone's privacy, even here, Mr. Arlen, I mean Arlen."

"Look, you are an agent, not a room clerk. This guy Pender is involved in something to do with Mrs. Toskini's death, and I know you don't think it was an accident, no matter what you once said. He also is a new arrival in this country from what Stan could tell from his language, so both of us should be interested in him. There is a slim chance that the address book may be in his room or that something else will come to hand. It's worth a try."

"Oh all right, we can go down there right now, while I've got someone watching the desk for me, but I can't be gone long. I'm pretty sure there are other people here who are involved."

They walked down the hall to Pender's door. It was ajar. Mia threw up her hand and stopped him. "Hold it a minute. Someone's in here."

Arlen moved up and pushed the door the rest of the way open. "You aren't kidding. Either that or Pender is a pretty sloppy housekeeper."

"Wait here and I'll go in and check it out," Mia whispered.

"Just go on in. Nobody's there now." Arlen pushed his walker past her and shuffled into the room, leaving Mia to follow.

"I wonder what else these guys wanted beside the address book." Mia walked over to the desk and stirred up the papers that were strewn on the floor. The drawers had been emptied and then thrown on top of the mess.

Arlen shuffled into the bathroom and saw that the medicine cabinet had been half torn off the wall. He looked inside, but it was empty. All the contents were spread across the counter and into the sink. He went back into the bedroom where Mia was shuffling through the papers that were thrown down on the bed.

"Find anything?"

She turned toward him and said, "No, I have no idea what to look for. We'd better leave. It's pretty obvious that someone else in this building is on the other side and I don't want them to know we are so interested in Pender. Come on, let's get out of here."

"Shouldn't we look over some of those papers that were in his desk?"

"No! We've been here too long as it is!" She turned and headed for the door. She opened it and stuck her head out, peering up and down the hall. "It's clear. Let's go. Go back to your room and I'll go to the elevators."

Arlen followed her out of the door and stopped at his door and watched her glide down the hall to the elevators. *Well, that didn't get us much,* he thought as he entered his room and closed the door behind him. The thought popped into his brain, *these guys seem to have easy access to all of our rooms. I don't like putting that chair up to my door. What if I fell and couldn't get up? I'd be stuck. Oh well, if I don't use the chair there's a good chance that I will fall down and not get up – ever.*

He didn't know why, but the thoughts made him pick up his grandma's Bible and lie down with it beside him.

He remembered that Stan had said, "This isn't like a regular book. You don't start at page one. Find the book of John, or Romans and start there."

That was pretty weird for a start. So he looked in the index until he eventually found the book called John and read for a while. A lot of it didn't make much sense to him, but he learned one thing. This guy called Jesus was no wimp. Somehow there were these guys at the Jewish temple who had a sweet deal going. They sold sacrificial animals and they changed real money for temple money. Jesus had come in one day and got mad when he saw the scam going on, so he drove the whole mess of them out into the street. It must have been sort of like driving the Mafia out of one of their casinos. He was going to have to see what Stan said about it. He guessed that working as a carpenter had made Jesus a pretty strong dude.

CHAPTER16

H e tossed the Bible on his bedside table and thought about what he had planned to do that day. He didn't know what the other inmates felt about it, but to him most of the activities Meadowview had planned for them seemed pretty infantile. *Well, perhaps some of us are back at that stage but just don't like to admit it*, he chuckled to himself. But take for example this morning's program, finger painting. What in the world would a grown man do with finger paints? He was only going because Betsy had told him at breakfast that she was going, and because he had to admit that he was getting pretty lonely. His room had begun to feel more like a cell again.

So at 10 AM they were all piling into the big room called 'The Rec Room', and several not so innocuous titles, down on the first floor. Actually it was a brightly-lighted square of a space, with big windows all along the west wall. This day there were a dozen of the famous folding tables scattered around. As he pushed his way into the middle of the room, he saw Betsy waving at him from one of the tables near the windows. She was wearing a shapeless blue smock that was already covered with brightly hued paint. *She must have started early*, he thought, as he headed toward her table.

"Hi, Mr. Arlen. Come on, I've saved a space for you." She pointed to a big white sheet that lay on the table, shining in its absence of any colors. Somehow he guessed he was supposed to make a magnificent work of art out of that pristine page. He saw several bowls of brightly colored paints arrayed in a row between their two sheets.

"Okay, how do I do it?"

"Well, you have such nice clothes on you had better go and get a smock." She pointed to the far wall, and he saw a whole line of smocks like the one she was wearing. Swallowing any pride he had left, he shuffled his way over to the wall and pulled one off of a hook and put it on over his polo shirt. He now knew how she had gotten paint on her smock before they started. All of the smocks had rainbow colors smeared all over them. As he walked back, Betsy smiled at him. He really thought she was trying to keep from laughing at him, but he gave her the benefit of a doubt.

As they put their hands into the messy paint and smeared it around over the white sheet, he felt a little like a fool. But he was surprised to find, after Mia had brought him over a chair so that he didn't have to balance on his walker, that the whole process was really soothing and therapeutic. He decided that he needed to remember that the Meadowview people had been at this business a lot longer than he had been here, and that perhaps some of the programs weren't as dumb as they seemed first off.

His reverie was broken as Betsy leaned over his shoulder to look at his red and yellow smears and say, "You are doing very well, Mr. Arlen. You have an artistic eye."

"I have to tell you the truth, Betsy, I almost didn't come to this thing. I thought it was only for the more senile among us. But I was wrong. I'm having a good time. Being here with you helps."

Betsy blushed red and said, "Oh, Mr. Arlen, I bet you say that to all the old ladies!" She laughed and patted his shoulder.

"No, I don't, just to the very nice young ones." He said. "I still haven't heard any more from that Devon character. Have you seen him around?"

Her face clouded up. "No, and that's strange. I was supposed to give him some final papers on my house yesterday, and he didn't show up. I wonder what happened."

"Well, the cops have been nosing around here some, and I told Lt. Crowder about him, so maybe he is lying low for a while. I haven't seen him, but I hadn't seen him before he invaded my room either. By the way, do you know anything about Mr. Pender who lives on the other side of me?"

"Oh, Mr. Arlen, you want to be careful of that man, too. He isn't very nice. He just about knocked me over going to the elevator the other day. And he speaks some funny language. It wasn't English at all."

"No, I believe he is from Eastern Europe or Asia, but I don't know what he is doing in this place. I do know that he and some of the other residents, you, for instance, don't seem to be old enough or helpless enough to be in here. He seems much younger and healthier than most of us."

He saw that Betsy suddenly got flustered, and she quickly changed the subject. "Mr. Arlen..."

He interrupted. "Please call me Arlen, Betsy. When you say Mr. Arlen, it seems like you are talking to my father."

"I'm sorry, Arlen, I keep forgetting. You seem like Mr. Arlen to me."

The rest of the morning went pretty fast, but Betsy didn't do much more talking. She withdrew and only seemed to mumble answers to his not so subtle questions, and when the instructor announced their noon break, she rushed out like her smock was on fire. She didn't come back for the afternoon session, so Arlen left early with his beautiful artwork unfinished.

Later as he pushed the button to raise the back of his bed, he decided that the day had given him more questions than answers. *What happened to nasty Devon? What had did I say that turned Betsy into a Sphinx? And why does it seem that the answer to all of those puzzles is just hanging out there waiting for me to grab it if I could let go of my walker long enough.* He didn't see how such a mild-mannered youngish woman like Betsy could be involved in all of this. But wait a minute! She is youngish. Why is she in this place? She seems young enough to be living on her own and the way she rushed out of the art program showed that she doesn't have any mobility problems. He raked his hand through his hair, moaned and lowered his bed back down, frustrated and tired.

CHAPTER 17

A sharp rap on the motel room door made him jump out of his chair.

"Who is?"

"Are you Max Pender?"

"No! Go away!"

"Mr. Pender, let us in. We came over from the church. We want to help you. We won't hurt you!"

"How you know my name?"

"Rev told us you are a neighbor of Mr. Arlen."

"Let us in Pender. We can't just stand out here yelling. Someone will call the cops!"

He knew when he heard that he would have to let them in. If they called the police he would be deported back to his jail cell for sure.

"OK, OK, a minute, please." He had bolted the door and so he reluctantly pulled back the bolt and pulled it open. As it swung back he stood facing two of the motorcycle men he had seen at the church. They looked very big and strong, but both of them were smiling. He hoped that was a good sign.

"Mr. Pender, we would like for you to come with us if you would. Rev would like to talk to you and to help you."

"Why would he want help me? He doesn't even know if I have problem."

"Most people who don't have a problem don't run out of church like their pants were on fire." The thin one laughed and patted him on the shoulder.

"So, even if he is right, I don't need religion, I need a place to hide. If you found me, those who want to hurt me can find me too."

"Hey, man, Rev isn't out to shove religion off on you or anyone else, and he can help you if anyone can. He has helped all of us in one way or another." The thin man sounded a little angry with him.

"I'm sorry. Okay, I go with you. What else I can do? Wait, I get my coat." He had a silly thought that he might get to ride on one of those big noisy motorcycles. He had never been on one before. But when they walked out into the parking lot all he saw was a beat up old pickup truck. They got in and the tall thin one slipped beneath the wheel and backed carefully out of the parking lot and aimed the truck down the street.

"Hey, we not going towards church!" he said in panic.

"Relax, Rev wants us to bring you to his house. He's got supper ready. He's a pretty good cook and he figured if we found you, you could probably use a good meal." This time it had been the short, stocky bearded man who explained it to him. He looked like he had enjoyed many of the reverend's good meals.

In a few minutes they stopped in front of a small white stucco house, and they all climbed out of the truck, and the thin man motioned him to follow them up the narrow sidewalk to the front door.

Max was startled when he walked into the house. The God-man looked entirely different. He was wearing a tan long sleeved shirt and his hair was combed down and just touched his collar.

"Come in and have a seat, Mr. Pender. I was hoping the boys would be able to find you in time for dinner." He motioned towards a long sofa that had seen much use.

"Why you send your men after me? I did nothing to you."
He refused the seat.

"No, No, of course not. I'm just hoping I can do something
for you. I know you live at Meadowview, and I know you
are in some kind of trouble. Go ahead and sit down. Dinner
is almost ready. Mr. Arlen says you weren't very nice to him,
but there must be some reason for that. You don't look like
a nasty person."

"How you know I'm not a nasty person?"

"I think you just need a little help. What did you do with
the address book?"

"I don't know what you talking about!" Max felt his face
getting red. He wasn't used to telling lies to priests.

"Of course you do. Mr. Arlen saw you drop it. He wanted
to talk to you, but you gave him the bum's rush and slammed
the door." The pastor was still smiling at him and that made
him more nervous. He didn't know what a 'bum's rush' was,
but it didn't sound very good and now he wished he hadn't
come there.

"Yes, you should have come. Now how can I help you if
you don't tell the truth? What happened to the address book?"

Max couldn't help noticing a sharper tone in the other's
voice. Besides it seemed like he could read his mind. He
knew he was sorry he had come, and he knew he was lying.
He decided he had to tell the truth to this God-man.

"Men took it. They came to my room and took it. I don't
have it any more."

"Who are the men?"

"I don't know men," he lied. "They know me though.
They know my name and where I live, and now I must move
and get away. They will come back. I thought motorcycle
men were them. I am very afraid."

"Lucky for you they weren't. Would you like to stay with
me while we get this thing straightened out? I have a spare
room that isn't being used. And the boys will be glad to go

over and pick your things up if you have any." His voice had become very gentle.

"I don't know. Why I should trust you? Maybe you are part of them, I don't know." His voice quavered.

"I understand your fear, Mr. Pender, but you are going to have to trust someone or you aren't going to make it. I don't know who those guys are, although I suspect you do, but they seem plenty tough and well-organized."

"They want kill me so I won't talk, but I don't know anything to talk about."

"Are they people you knew before you moved into Meadowview?"

Max wondered if the God-man would understand how badly he wanted to get to this country. And did he have any idea how hard it would have been for him if he had stayed in Tajikistan?

"I had some business dealings with those who employ them. I have seen men before in an office."

Stan sat down on the sofa beside him and said, "Mr. Pender, unless we can stop these men, they are going to hurt others like you and like my grandma and none of you will be safe. Why don't you sit back and tell me about it."

Max had never been around a man who was so persuasive and assuring. So he found himself telling him about Dushanbe and how he still had to get his Anna out and how the men had helped him, and how Anna and he had given them most of their money and more for forged papers. He told him that he thought that if only he could make it to America, he could make lots of money and that soon he would have his Anna back, but now he would never see her again. The God-man listened well. He really seemed to want to know about him. It's too bad he can't really help.

"Max, I think you've had enough for one day. Why don't I show you where your room is, and you can get freshened up and we'll have a bite to eat and go to bed." He rose and took Max's arm and led him to the back of the house.

"This room should do," he said, pushing open a door in the hallway. "It's not fancy, but it has got a good bed. We'll talk some more later."

An hour later Max decided to lie down on the bed for a minute before he got undressed and he immediately fell asleep. It had been a long, hard day.

CHAPTER 18

A rlen was beginning to think that the phone rang too much. He had been sound asleep and now it seemed as if the phone was trying to jump off his bedside table. He wished he could turn the tone down, but wasn't sure that it would wake him up unless it was good and loud. "Arlen here," he mumbled.

"Hi, Arlen, it's Stan. I've got a surprise for you. You gonna be home in a few?"

"Sure, I'm not sleeping now anyway, come on over."

A few minutes later the loud knock on the door told him that Stan had hurried.

"Hi, Arlen," he said as he strode through the door Arlen had just opened. "I've got some interesting news." He strolled over and plunked down on Arlen's bed.

Arlen shuffled over and sat down beside him. "I've got a little news too, but tell me yours first."

"No, go ahead, mine will wait."

"Well, OK. Did you know that Mia is an INS special agent?"

"No, but it figures."

"Why is that?"

"Tell you in a minute. Go ahead with your story."

"She and I have been talking about Pender and the address book, and we decided to check out his room because he seems to be missing. It had been professionally trashed. We looked around a little, but were afraid he would come back, or that someone might be watching us, so we left. We need to look around in there some more. So far the guy hasn't come home."

Stan laughed and Arlen got a little sore. He didn't think the story was particularly funny.

Toskini raised his hand and said, "Sorry, but I think it's time for me to tell you my news. Pender is at my house sleeping as we speak. The guys collected him this afternoon at a motel near the church. He came into the church, but got spooked and ran out. It wasn't much of a problem for Rocks and Toby to find him. It's their neighborhood. I don't think he really is a tough guy, just an immigrant with phony papers who is deathly afraid he will get sent back to a jail cell in the old country."

"Sounds like we're beginning to get a glimmer here. If Mia is doing an INS investigation and Pender is here on phony papers, we need to get them together and see what happens."

Stan held up a restraining hand and said, "No, I don't think so. I promised I would protect Pender while he is at my home, and I'm not going to turn him over to the INS until I know what is going to happen to him. They would just pack him up and send him back."

Arlen stood up and faced him, "But he may be the key to the whole thing, your grandma's death and everything. You can't hide him from that. Besides, if he's in the country illegally, he'll have to go back sooner or later."

Stan looked at Arlen, a calm peace radiating from his upraised face. "Maybe so, but I'm not going to be the one who blows the whistle on him. He came to me for sanctuary, so I'm begging you to give me some time with him so I can figure out how to help him. His wife is still in the old country and he is pretty stressed out."

"This is getting way too deep. I promised Mia I would help her find him, and now you are asking me to hide the fact that I know where her best witness is stashed. I don't know if I can do that."

"All I ask is that you give me a few days. I won't hide him forever. In the meantime, I will keep questioning him and see if I can find out any more about those people who are hunting for him. I think he is just a small pawn in a big game of some kind. You had better lay low and stay out of trouble. I'll keep working on it because I can run faster than you can!" He laughed again, stood up, started towards the door and then turned around and said, "How about joining me in a prayer. The Bible says that where two or three are gathered in His Name, He is there with them."

Arlen was really embarrassed, and when the other man grabbed both of his hands he almost pulled away, but then he shrugged and said, "Go ahead."

"Father, you know we want to solve this mystery, and you know we don't want to harm those who have been forced to do things against their wills. Guide us, and give Arlen and me wisdom that will help us in a manner that is pleasing to you. In Jesus' Name, Amen." He released Arlen's hands, waved and left the room.

When Arlen had gotten over his embarrassment at being pulled into Stan's prayer, his reporter's crazy bone began to itch. He decide that he had just thought up a new mixed metaphor, but despite that, he knew he wanted to get into Pender's room again, and he wasn't sure he wanted Mia there when he did it.

He had always denied it, but over his years as an investigative reporter, he had learned a few shady tricks. One of them was how to break into a locked room. He pushed his walker over to his own door and opened it and looked at the lock. No wonder somebody had been able to break into his room. It looked like the kind of lock that could be opened with a credit card. Meadowview must have counted on security at the front door and not internally. *Well,* he thought, *it's worth a try.* And, while he was up and at his door seemed like the best time to give it a shot. So he pushed his walker out the door and down the hall. He wondered if he could still do it. He had a nice, newish Discover Card that he only used when he had enough money to consider using a card, which wasn't often. He slid it into the crack in the door and wiggled it a little and the door popped open at his push. He was in!

He had to be pretty careful because all the contents of the dresser were still on the floor. It would be pretty bad if he fell in this room and they found him there lying on top of Pender's stuff. He didn't think he could explain that. He shook himself out of his scary thoughts and started looking around. He had heard that if you stand still at the entrance to a room and scan it systematically, you can spot anything unusual or out of order in it.

Arlen had to laugh as he tried that, because everything was out of order in this room. He decided he would try the desk first. He figured the goons who had searched it before him knew what they were doing, but maybe if they found what they were looking for, whatever that was — they already had the book — they didn't stay around. But since he didn't have any idea of what he was looking for, he probably didn't have sense enough to quit.

He picked up the desk chair that was lying sideways on top of two over-turned drawers and sat down. He picked up the first drawer and saw only a pile of pencils and paperclips lying on the floor. Nothing exciting there. The space under the second drawer yielded only a few small tablets and some number ten envelopes stacked neatly on the carpet. The guys must have been pretty sure of what they were looking for. They hadn't even riffled through the piles.

One of the tablets looked a little different than the other two. He couldn't figure it out, but it looked like it was foreign. He first dismissed the idea, because he knew that most things like that come from foreign countries these days, but this one just didn't look like it was made for use in this country. As he picked it up, he spied some notes in some sort of Cyrillic script.

He was about to toss the book back down when a page of Cyrillic words slid out from between two pages. Beside some of the words was the same kind of moon/handle mark that had been in Mrs. Toskini's address book. He had hit the jackpot, but he couldn't cash it in because the reward was in foreign coin. He stuck the page into his pocket and looked around until his back and legs told him to go home, and he hadn't found anything else of any interest.

So he dragged himself back to his room and flopped down on his bed. As he relaxed his body, his mind pondered the problem until a quick solution popped into his head. He actually knew a guy who might be able to decipher the page. He had met him when he used to work at the newspaper. His name even came to mind after a minute's thought. Alec Trotsky! *With that name,* he thought, *he must know a lot about Russia.* He laughed out loud and decided he would have to call him tomorrow. Until then, he was going to sleep, and as he drifted off he thought, *Pender doesn't quite sound Russian,* but he would bet that the language on that page was.

CHAPTER 19

"Oh, Arlen, I just heard that Mr. Pender is missing! What do you suppose in going on?"

"I don't know, Betsy. Mia just told me he hasn't come back home after he went out with a couple of men the other night. I don't know much about it."

They were sitting in the dining room before breakfast time. It was too early for Arlen, but Betsy had said that she came down early every morning for a cup of coffee. He had struggled with a lot of muscle pain that night, and had decided he just couldn't stay in bed any longer, so he had wandered down and spotted her there. It was nice to see her. She was a bright spot in a dim day.

"Well, Arlen, you are a real good reporter. I thought you might have just been checking around a bit. You reporters are really perceptive and can usually see what's going on around you."

Arlen was flattered by her praise and decided it wouldn't hurt to tell her a little about what was going on, although he wasn't sure he knew very much. But he wouldn't tell her too much, because his big mouth often got him into trouble.

"Well, just between you and me, I'm pretty sure that Mr. Pender is up to no good. He had an address book that belonged to Mrs. Toskini and now someone has trashed his room looking for something else."

"Oh my, whatever were they looking for?"

"I wish I knew, and I also wish I knew if they had found it. His room was pretty messed up."

"Were you in his room?" she smiled a conspiratorial grin and reached out and touched his arm.

A strong feeling pulsed through him at her touch, but he said, "Oops, I knew my big mouth would get me into trouble. Yes, I sneaked in there last night, but I didn't find anything. Everything was too messed up." He didn't mention the paper he had found.

"I knew it! You are still a reporter. You have to find things out. That's so exciting! But be careful. I sure don't want to see you hurt."

"I'm trying to stay out of trouble, but it seems to follow me around." He was flattered that she was worried about him. It had been awhile since someone had really cared.

Now that he was back in his room and had a minute to think, he realized that he would have to be more careful what he said. He had almost blurted out Mia's real job here, and that could be disastrous for her. He had been so taken with talking to Betsy that he had paid no attention to who was sitting around them, or of any of the serving people coming and going. Betsy didn't seem to be the type to spread stories, but someone in the place must be working for whoever killed Mrs. Toskini, and who knows, if it wasn't Pender, it might have been a server or even one of the kitchen volunteers. Dumb! Dumb!

He was just settling down in his desk chair when the phone jangled. Of course he had moved it over beside the bed, so he had to struggle up and shuffle over to his bedside table. He dropped down on the edge of the mattress and said, "Arlen here."

"Hello, Mr. Arlen."

"Oh, hi, Lieutenant. What's up?"

"You know that tough boy, Devon, who was trying to boost your property?"

"Yeah, I have been expecting him to come and growl at me some more. He doesn't seem to be around."

"Well, you don't have to worry about him anymore. We found him in the lake this morning. He had been shot once in the middle of the forehead."

"If this keeps up, Lieutenant, you are going to believe me about Mrs. Toskini."

"I believe you. But it still seems funny that someone would do in an innocent old lady."

"I agree, but I think you and I had better talk again. I know a few things that you might be interested in. Can you come over sometime today?"

"Yeah, I have to be over that way to check out Devon's room and stuff. Be there about eleven o'clock. Would you like to look at his room with me?"

"Well of course. I thought you'd never ask." After he hung up, Arlen began to worry. It seemed that things just kept getting more muddled. At least he didn't have to fight over his little piece of property until Meadowview sent another tough guy to take Devon's place. But what in the world did Meadowview's tough guy have to do with Mia's case, or even Mrs. Toskini's murder? And why did he never see him if he lived at Meadowview?

"What a disappointment!" Arlen said, "Devon's room looks as if it had never been lived in."

"It is pretty obvious that it isn't his main abode," the lieutenant answered.

The modern white dresser contained only about two changes of clothes. There was only one jacket in the closet and not a picture or a magazine not even a scrap of paper in the wastebasket. Mia had come down to the first floor room with them. She looked pretty interested, but was trying hard to seem bored. He didn't think the lieutenant was buying it.

"Miss Carson, what did this guy do at Meadowview?" Lt. Crowder turned and glared at her.

"I think he was with the corporate accounts people. He was here before I came. He wasn't around most of the time. I assumed that he worked at all the regional facilities. He said he was in charge of protecting the company's assets."

"Boy, was he ever!" Arlen couldn't help exclaiming.

"Yes, he wasn't too nice. When I first got here I tried to get the company to keep him away from us, but they didn't seem to even know what I was talking about, so I figured he was in some special department and let it go. I was new and didn't know all the ins and outs."

"Well, he ended up in the lake with a hole in his skull. What do you think caused that?" he shot back at her.

"I don't know, Lieutenant. I didn't know the man very well. He made a pass at me once and after I dealt with that, he didn't talk to me. He certainly didn't confide in me!"

"Miss Carson, I have been told your real identity and I would like to point out to you that we can both do better if we cooperate. If there is anything you should be telling me, now would be an excellent time to do so."

Mia turned and frowned at Arlen, "I understand that, Lieutenant, but we are investigating two different things. I don't know that they are related."

Arlen interrupted, "I didn't tell him!"

"I still would appreciate knowing what you have found out and what direction you are heading." His voice hadn't softened.

"I will be as cooperative as I can, but you are investigating a local crime or several crimes, and I believe I am into an international operation. I don't think they overlap very much." The ice in her voice hadn't melted. Arlen was hearing a side of both of them that he had never heard before.

"Okay, but I think they are tied together like two strands of the same rope. I find my man or men and you will find your international organization. Let's just leave it at that." With that blast, he turned and strode out of the room.

"That was a bit much, wasn't it?" Arlen asked Mia when they were alone. He thought, *so much for getting anything out of the lieutenant today!*

"Arlen, you just don't know how big this thing we are following may be." Her voice softened and the icy glare melted.

"That's as may be, but you didn't need to get so nasty and superior about it. Crowder is a good guy and he's just trying to do his job."

"That may be true, but we've already uncovered ties to their organization in at least three different police forces. I just can't afford to compromise my job more than it already has been by my people admitting to him who I am. I have to say though, at this point we haven't gotten very far, and I wish I could get some help."

"Do you think Devon had anything to do with your case, or was he just in the wrong place at the wrong time?" Arlen had to sit down in the only chair in the room.

"I wish I knew. I have been watching him for a while, but he never seemed to do anything but harass the guests. He was a nasty piece of work."

"Maybe he found out what was going on with Mrs. Toskini and Max Pender and someone didn't like it. It sounds like he was executed in real professional style."

"I have been checking on who really owns Meadowview and that isn't very easy either. They seem to be owned by a holding company that in turn is under the wing of an international real estate cartel and from there the trail gets real fuzzy. My people are still trying to find the end of the pipeline. That might give us a clue, but I can't wait. I need to figure out what is going on, and Devon getting killed doesn't help."

CHAPTER 20

A rlen was late for lunchtime as he headed down from his room, still pondering his mixed loyalties. As he reached the door of the dining room he saw that Betsy was standing by the door gazing down the hall.

"Hi, Arlen, I've been waiting for you. Come on." She took his arm and led him to a table in the middle of the room. She helped him sit down and folded up his walker and pulled her chair close to him.

"What have you been doing all morning, Arlen dear?"

"Oh nothing much." He hated lying to her, but they were in the middle of a crowded room and he remembered his big mouth the last time they had talked.

"Did you hear? One of the maids said that she had heard that that nasty Devon man had been murdered. Have you heard about that?" She clutched his arm and shook it excitedly.

"Well, yes, but I didn't think anyone else knew about it. I guess you can't keep anything quiet in this place." He was enjoying the touch of her hand.

"Oh, she said, quickly removing her hand from his arm. "I didn't know it was a secret. I'm sorry I said anything. I've told a couple of people because they had been threatened by that nasty man."

"No, that's all right, it will probably be in the papers this afternoon anyway. He was found in the lake with a bullet in his head."

"In the same lake where poor Mr. Bozeman was found?"

"I guess so, they didn't say. But I think we could talk about something a little more pleasant than murder. What have you been doing to while away the hours?"

"I'm still in the painting class three days a week. It's very relaxing. I don't think I'm very good at it, but they hung one of my paintings in the hall and that embarrassed me. I don't think it's that good."

"I'll bet it's great!" He seemed to always be stretching the truth when he was talking to this lady, but he really wanted to have her as a friend. "I know my effort was pretty poor, so I haven't been back. Maybe I'll come and try it again tomorrow. I kind of had the idea last time that you were pretty upset with me for some reason. You sort of clammed up on me and then left in a hurry."

"I'm sorry, Arlen...I wasn't feeling well and the thought of that mean Mr. Devon didn't help. And you talked about me being younger, and yet I still can't take care of myself. That hurt me, so I ran off. I'm fine now, and I'm so sorry that you thought I was mad at you. I wasn't mad at all." She shyly touched his arm again. He wasn't going to miss that class for anything, now.

It didn't take him long to realize that his painting in this class wasn't any better than the first one. The mess on the paper in front of him looked like the product of a three-year-old orangutan. Of course, the orangutan was probably better at it. The only plus was that Betsy was there beside him and her soft voice and frequent pats on the arm kept him going.

He turned to her and said, "I' really appreciate having you to talk to. I am pretty confused about Mrs. Toskini's death and now Devon's murder. I do better when I can talk about it." At first she had seemed a little ditzy, but after they got to talking, he could see that she was a lot smarter than she let on.

"Oh, Arlen, I'm so glad I can help you. I don't like to talk about it, but I don't mind listening to you. You seem so smart. I'm sure you will get it figured out."

"I'm not doing so hot so far. I hope nobody else gets killed."

"I hope not too. Let's talk about something else."

They chatted for a while and her final advice was the same as her first, "don't get involved."

He felt ready to take her advice. He kept writing down everything he had learned and then throwing away the list because it wasn't much different than the previous one. He still hadn't told Mia that Pender was staying with Stan Toskini. He was sure that she wouldn't be very happy if she found out, but he had promised Stan to give him some time, so he hadn't decided to blow the whistle yet. He wasn't sure what he was waiting for; the thought of hiding something that important from her really made him uncomfortable.

CHAPTER 21

"Good evening, sir. Are you alone?" The maître'd smiled at Arlen.

"Yes, it's just me."

"Follow me, and I will find you a nice table."

Arlen followed the greeter into the small restaurant, embarrassed to have to push his walker past the filled tables. The greeter seated him in a small booth near the door so he didn't have to walk very far.

I don't think this is a good idea, he thought. *I wish I hadn't promised Stan I would do it. I feel like an old cripple. I suppose all these people are looking at me and feeling sorry for me.*

But when his dinner came he was glad he had come. The food was good and it was different than any of the menus at Meadowview, which was his point in coming.

A man walked up to his table and smiled. "You're from Meadowview, aren't you?"

Arlen frowned at him and said, "Yes, how did you know?"

"I'm from there, too. I live down on the first floor. I've seen you at meals."

"Sorry, I didn't recognize you. Would you care to sit down?"

"I've already had my meal, but I'll sit a minute. Do you have a way to get back home?"

"I'll just take a cab."

The man shook his head. "No need to do that, I've got my car out in the parking lot. I'll be glad to take you home when you are finished."

Arlen stood up and pulled out his wallet. "I'm done, just let me go up and pay my bill, and I'll be happy to get a ride. By the way, what's your name? Mine's Arlen."

"Hi, Arlen. I'm Bill. Go ahead and pay. I'll wait for you at the door."

Arlen shuffled up to the counter and paid his tab and then pushed his walker over to the front door, and they went out together. They didn't speak until they got into the small parking lot.

"That's my car over there. Go ahead and get in, and I'll put your walker in the back seat."

Arlen slid into the passenger seat and handed his walker to Bill. After the walker was stowed, Bill jumped into the driver's seat and drove out of the lot.

"Are you familiar with our parks, Arlen? I usually drive through our arboretum on the way home. Mind if we go that way?"

"No. I'm in no hurry to get back. It might be nice."

Bill didn't answer, but swung the car off the main road and down a residential street. He drove on for about a mile and then entered a tree-lined street.

Arlen said, "I've never been here before. I didn't even know it existed."

Bill smiled and said, "You will get to know it better tonight. There's a place I want to show you if you've never been here. It's just down the road. We'll have to get out of the car to see it, but it is well worth it. We can get there before dark."

He drove on without saying anything more and then swung the car down a narrow side street and drove to the end of the dead-end road, turned around and drove back a ways and stopped. "It's right off the road here. Go ahead and get out, and I will park and then get your walker out."

Arlen looked around and didn't see anything special, but he opened the door and shuffled out onto the street. Immediately Bill yelled at him, "Quit being so snoopy or you'll get worse next time!" and roared off, leaving Arlen standing in the street without his walker.

He tried to sit down on the low curb and fell over on his side. He lay there trying to figure out what he could do. *I can't walk out of here,* he thought, *and no one will be coming in here this late in the day. I think I'm stuck.*

The sun was setting and the air began to run chills up and down his arms. He tried to stand up and walk, but after only a few feet his balance threw him over on the pavement again.

Later that evening the clerk at the front desk at Meadowview picked up the phone and dialed Mia's number. "Hi, Mia. I just thought I'd better tell you, Mr. Arlen hasn't come back from going out to dinner. It seems to me he should have been back by now. He went out alone, so it shouldn't have taken him so long."

"Maybe he stopped to take in a movie or something."

"I don't think so. When he left he told me he was just going out to dinner. I think something happened to him."

"Okay, I'll be down in a minute." Mia pulled her shoes on and started out the door. Then she stopped and picked up her cell phone and dialed 911.

"Emergency services. Do you have an emergency?"

"I think so. I am in charge of Meadowview Assisted Living Center, and one of our guests went out to dinner and hasn't come back. He should have been back several hours ago."

"Are you sure he didn't go to a movie or a nightclub or something?"

"He told our desk clerk he was just going out to dinner. He walks with a walker, so I don't believe he would be very active. I'm pretty sure he will need some help."

"Please give me all the information you can."

After Mia had hung up she looked in her phone's address book and called Lt. Crowder.

"Crowder residence."

"Hi. This is Mia Carson, down at Meadowview. May I speak to Lt. Crowder?"

She filled the lieutenant in, and he said he would run downtown and would see what he could find out.

Lt. Crowder stood up and said, "Honey, I've got to go downtown. Don't know how long I'll be gone. One of Meadowview's people have gone missing. I need to see if we can find him."

"Oh, do you have to go? I just made us some popcorn. I thought we could watch a movie."

"I'm sorry. You shouldn't have married a cop. I'll be back as soon as I can. Go on and watch your movie." He bent over and kissed her, grabbed his keys off the counter and hurried out the door.

Back in the park Arlen was shivering all over. He tried lying down on the pavement, but quickly decided that wasn't a good idea. There were no street lights on the side street so it just kept getting darker. Soon he began to feel faint and had to struggle to sit up on the curb. He slapped his arms to try to get some circulation back into his body, but had to stop when he almost fainted again.

I wish I believed in Toskini's god. I could use him now. I think I'm done for. No one will drive down this road until tomorrow. That will be too late. Oh no! His eyes closed and he fell over on his side on the pavement, unconscious.

"Lieutenant, we got all the units we can spare out looking for him. It's a big town. We got it divided up, but it will take us a while to get around it. Besides, he's probably inside somewhere."

"Did you check the hospitals?"

"Sure, we checked every place we thought he might be. We think we found the restaurant that he was in. The lady said she thought he went out with another man.we just aren't sure that was him."

"Well, keep looking. If somebody picked him up there's no telling where he is."

Lt. Crowder picked up his cell phone and dialed Stan Toskini. "Hi, Stan, Lt. Crowder here. Arlen is missing. He was supposed to go out to a restaurant to eat and he never came home. Have you heard anything from him?"

"No. He called me earlier and asked me if I knew any good inexpensive restaurants. I recommended one. Maybe he went there. It is the Feed Bag down on main."

"Okay, that's the one where they spotted a man with a walker. That must have been him. But they said he went out with another man. That doesn't make sense because he was alone."

"I'll get my guys right on it, lieutenant, they will find him."

"That's a good idea. Let me know what you find."

Ten minutes later the roar of big bike engines reverberated through the still town.

Twenty five riders divided the town up and soon were waking up neighborhoods with the roar of their exhausts, as they tore up and down the streets. Rocks sped down one side street and saw a flash of blue lights bouncing off his rearview mirror. He pulled over and stopped. A motorcycle officer strode up to him and pulled out his ticket book.

"You were going pretty fast, sir. This is a 25mph zone. May I see your license?"

"Sorry, man. We are looking for a man who may be down and we think that every minute counts. He is handicapped and can't walk out for help."

"You looking for Mr. Arlen?"

"Yeah, you guys looking for him?"

"We are, but it's a big city and we need all the help we can get. I won't ticket you, but please slow it down a bit and try to be a little quieter in these residential neighborhoods. We will get lots of phone calls tomorrow complaining about you evil bikers."

"Okay, sir, I'm sorry I made so much noise. I was really concentrating on finding Arlen. Someone could have carried him off, but we will find him. I only hope it's not too late."

"Good luck. I may see you again along the route. Be sure to let us know if you find him." He waved and turned and strolled back to his own motorcycle.

Rocks picked up his CB microphone and said, "hey, Toby. Any luck?"

"Nah, I'm over on the west side. If he's here he's inside somewhere. Think the bad guys got him?"

"I'm not sure. Talk to your contacts and let me know if there is any word going around." He pushed the starter and headed down the street, driving slowly and as quietly as his bike would let him.

Four hours later he checked in with Lt. Crowder, but no one had seen Arlen since he left the restaurant. "It's looking like someone took him somewhere and has him inside." Crowder said.

"I got my guys checking their sources to see if anyone knows anything, but they haven't heard a word about him. I'm afraid it's going to be too late when we find him. I only got one more place to look. I'm almost out of town. I am going to take a quick spin through the arboretum. I don't have much hope that he would be there, but we've looked pretty nearly everywhere else."

"Okay, Rocks. Let me know what you find. I'm really worried about him. He has crossed some really mean people."

Rocks started his bike again and turned into the tree lined street that was the entrance to the park. It was so dark that he just crawled along straining his eyes to see along the sides of the tree covered streets. He saw a side street, and for no reason he could later think of, he turned down the street. He stared to the right and to the left, but couldn't see much of anything. It turned out to be a dead-end street, so he turned around and headed back out, moving a little faster. Halfway back to the main street he spotted something alongside of the road. He swung over and shone his headlight on it and saw a man lying curled up on the curb. He slammed on the brakes, leaped off his bike and raced over and knelt by the man.

"Arlen! Arlen! Can you hear me?" He sat down on the cold cement and ripped his jacked off and threw it over Arlen, tucking it in around his body. He put his legs out and lifted Arlen's head up and placed it on his knee and felt his neck for signs of a pulse. *Thank you, Lord, he's alive. Not very much alive, but I can feel a little pulse. Please keep him alive, dear God.*

He pulled out his phone and punched in 911. When he was assured that the paramedics were on the way he dialed Lt. Crowder. "I found him. He's way out here in the arboretum. He's still alive, but barely. I got the paramedics on the way."

"Great! I'm not far from there. I'm in my car. I'll try and make it as fast as I can. Don't mess around with anything. I'll see if there is any evidence in the area."

"Fine. When you get about the middle of the main road in the park there's a small road that goes off to the left. He's about half way down that road, on the left side. I left my bike's lights on so you will see it."

Less than five minutes later a black and white, with its lights flashing into the night roared up beside Rock's bike and squealed to a stop. Lt. Crowder jumped out and ran over to where Rocks was sitting on the curb holding Arlen.

Sunlight was streaming through the window of the hospital room when Arlen began to feel his body again. He tried to open his eyes, but the glare blinded him so he closed them. All he knew was that he was warm. It seemed to him that he had never been warm before. He lapsed back into a never never land, half asleep and half awake. Finally, he heard some noises around him and felt a jab in his wrist. He jerked it away from the jab and heard a female voice say, "don't do that. I need to put this IV in."

His eyes popped open and he saw a women standing beside him. She was in a brightly colored scrub jacket and was smiling at him. The bright scrubs hurt his eyes.

"I'm glad you're awake, but don't fight me. You are pretty dehydrated, so we are hydrating you. That makes sense, doesn't it?" She chuckled.

"What am I doing here?"

"A deep voice said, "You decided to go to the park and sleep out on the sidewalk. But you forgot to bring your sleeping bag, so you got a little chilly."

His head jerked around and he saw Rocks overwhelming a small guest chair.

"What you doing here? Did Stan tell you to keep me out of trouble?"

Rocks chuckled. "You got yourself into all the trouble you needed. I found you out on the side of a dead-end road in the arboretum. Don't you remember being there?"

Arlen started to say, "No..." but then he stopped. "Yeah. It's coming back. I went to a restaurant, and a guy said he was from Meadowview and offered to give me a ride home. Boy, was I stupid. The guy couldn't have been over 40 years old. He wasn't from Meadowview."

"Well, I think you'd better not think about it for a while. When Lt. Crowder hears that you are awake he will be here asking you more questions than you ever will want to answer. I'm going to go now that I know you are okay, but I just want to leave you with something to think about. I was looking for you on the main road. I would never have turned down that little side road, but I got a strong message that I should go that way. I went clear down to the dead-end and didn't find

148

you so I turned back. Then I spotted you. That was the Lord's doing, not mine. So you'd better lift your voice to heaven and thank Him. He is the one that kept you alive. Goodbye." He got up and started toward the door.

"Thanks, Rocks. I owe my life to you, and I won't forget it. And I don't know much about your God, but I am trying to learn. I will get Stan to help me to know how to thank Him, because I know you are right. But don't belittle what you did. You and your pals were out in the middle of a cold night burning up the streets just to find me. Again, thanks."

Rocks didn't answer, he just waved his hand and left the room in a hurry.

"You better listen to your friend, sir," the nurse said. "We were told that you were down on that cold sidewalk for over six hours and yet you are in remarkably good shape. You will surely be able to go home today. Human resources couldn't have done that."

"I'm sure you are right. I'm just not used to there really being a God that cares for me. I wrote too many articles ridiculing those who believed in Him, but still he took care of me. It is going to take me a while to figure it all out."

That afternoon as he was lying in his comfortable bed in Meadowview he had reason to remember Rocks' warning about Lt. Crowder. His head was spinning from trying to answer all the questions.

CHAPTER 22

As he shuffled down the hall to the dining room, he decided that the Meadowview's food was really good and that he should be more thankful. *Especially after my experience at a restaurant,* he thought. His appetite had picked up and he could still eat just about anything. He knew that some of his fellow inmates couldn't do that. As he reached the dining room, he spied Betsy waving at him from what he came to think of their table. He ate with her almost every night. Tonight she seemed to have dressed up for some reason. She wore a bright print dress with an open collar which she had decorated with a bright scarf held on one shoulder by a gold pin in the shape of an angel. Her light hair was styled to frame her round face and two gold angel earrings peeked out from the curls over her ears.

"Hi, Arlen, dear. How are you doing today? Are you over your frightful night?"

"I'm fine. It's been a pretty slow day."

"No progress on the case? I bet you are disappointed."

"I think I'm about to take your advice and drop the whole thing. I don't ever seem to make any headway, and I don't think the police are doing much."

"That fat lieutenant doesn't seem very smart, does he?"

"He's smart enough, it's just a complicated case."

"What makes it so complicated? Do they think Mr. Devon's death is linked to Mrs. Toskini's? I don't see how that could be."

"Well, it is complicated because..." He had almost blurted out Mia's real identity. He started again, "It may not be so complicated, I guess all murders are tough to solve." He hoped his face hadn't turned red while he was talking.

"I'm sure that's true, but weren't you going to say something else?"

"Oh, I was just going to say how baffled I am, but that embarrassed me so I decided not to say it. I am feeling pretty dumb."

She grabbed his arm. "You're not dumb at all. You just have no way to get the facts. Just leave it to the officers. I don't want you to get hurt again." She dropped his arm and continued, "I guess that Mr. Pender is really gone, Arlen, dear. He still hasn't come back. I'm glad. He seemed like a nasty man." They were sitting enjoying hot apple pie alamode. It was getting dark outside and most of the diners had left the dining room. A small group was clustered around the coffee urn chatting before going off to their rooms.

"Don't worry about Mr. Pender, Betsy. He can take care of himself. He may not be as bad as we think he is. Other people seem to think that he is just hiding from something."

"Who thinks that, dear?" She touched his bare arm again, sending shock waves through his system.

"Stan Toskini, for one."

"Well, Stan is a dear, but you know how some of those pastors are, they see good in everyone. I still think he is a bad man." She removed her hand and frowned at him. "You must be careful."

"You may be right, but since he isn't here, I'm not going to worry about him." The thought flashed through his mind, *I haven't heard from Toskini. I don't even know if Pender is still there. Boy, I've got to be more careful what I think and say. I could blurt out all sorts of stuff to her.*

They moved on to more pleasant subjects and pretty soon it was time for him to shuffle back to his room. It always picked his spirits up to spend time with Betsy and before they parted they decided that they would go together to the barbecue that Meadowview was throwing on their back patio the next night. He hated to think it, but he was really getting pretty well adjusted to the assisted living lifestyle.

As he lay on his bed, he spent an hour or so reading his grandma's Bible and a couple of small booklets that Stan had dropped on his desk. He began to get a weird feeling that there was more to this religion stuff than merely religion. He was finding out that it was a lot different than what he had been told by people who obviously didn't know any more about it than he did. Then he remembered his recent conversation with Stan.

"I don't understand how something that was alleged to have happened 2,000 years ago to a non-descript Hebrew could possibly have any meaning for the world today. And I get really ticked at those religious fanatics who try and tell me that the world is only 6,000 years, old and that it somehow popped into being because some deity said so. All the scientists know that we came out of some primordial goop millions of years ago. It just built up and changed a little at a time until there was us. It sure makes sense to me." He frowned a little because he sometimes wondered down in his depths if it really did make sense.

Stan just smiled and said, "That's just because you don't read the right books. But I don't care about that right now, Arlen, I'm a lot more interested in showing you how that 2000-year-old non-descript Hebrew guy fits into your life today. Do you ever do things you wish you hadn't? What we call sin?"

"Well sure. I make mistakes. Everyone does. That's just part of life." He shrugged, feeling a little uncomfortable as a few of his real clinkers raced through his mind.

"That's why Jesus came. To offer you forgiveness for those sins."

"Why do I need that?"

"Because, before long, you and I will be standing before the eternal judge and, if they aren't hidden in the blood of Christ, you will have to answer for them"

Arlen chuckled, but at the same time, a small shudder ran through his body.

"Oh now we're back to the big grand-daddy who made us all. But I told you, I don't believe in him."

"One day you will, Arlen, one day you will. Read your Bible, and if you think about it while you're reading it, you will find that it is the one thing that makes perfect sense."

CHAPTER 23

H e woke up thinking how glad he was that he had the phone moved. It seemed to ring at the most ungodly hours. It was only 7 AM and it was trying to jump off of the table.

"Arlen here."

"Hi, Arlen, Stan Toskini. I hope I didn't wake you up, but I have some new news. Pender ran off again. He thought someone was looking for him last night and he got spooked. I don't know where he is now."

"Did you see anyone prowling around?" Arlen sat up and stretched his sore muscles.

"No, I wasn't looking, but Pender never quit looking out the window or peeking out the back door. The guy was really spooked."

"Well, I think the bad guys aren't the only ones after him. The INS is pretty interested in him. I don't know if Mia knows that he has phony papers, but I guess I'll have to ask her."

"Well, if he shows up back there, let me know. I still think I might be able to help him if he'll let me. He sure is scared."

After he hung up, he found himself again in a state of flux about Mia. He had decided to trust her and had told her so, but what if she was a phony? Experts in his long career had fooled him. Sometimes he hadn't been good at sorting the wheat from the chaff, and he remembered some of his poorer columns that had proved it.

He finally frowned at his own wishy-washy brain and told himself that he didn't really have much choice but to trust her, at least for now.

He got out of bed and dressed, wishing that he had a computer and a scanner so that he could send the page he had found to Alec, but he knew he would have to take it to him. Stan still wasn't getting around real well, and besides, he had to find ways to do more for himself. He decided that he could afford a cab for this trip.

It was the first time he had been back in the newspaper office since they had retired him out the door. It looked much the same, but the big desktop computers had all been replaced by laptops and tablets, which were spread out on the still cluttered desks. He quickly decided that a laptop was something he was going to have. They were fine.

As he threaded his way through the battered desks to Alec's spot in the corner, he didn't recognize a single staffer. And he noticed how young they all looked. *Well*, he thought, *it's a young people's game anyway. Too much stress, worry and too many deadlines for us old guys.* But somewhere deep inside the thought percolated up to the surface of his brain that he would give a lot to still be doing it with them.

Alec came out to greet him. "Hi, Arlen. Does this feel like coming home?"

Arlen smiled. "For just a minute it made me want to be back here. Then I remembered deadlines. The place is still a mess, even with laptops."

"Well, come on into the break room and we'll see what we will see."

As they settled down in the uncomfortable chairs that sprawled around the small table Alec said, "Let me see the paper you want me to read. I like mysteries." He held out his hand.

"Well, it isn't much, but it may help us if we know what it says. While you are at it, take a gander at that little symbol that is beside some entries, and see if you recognize it." He handed over the small piece of paper and sat back in his chair. Alec grabbed a pen out of his pocket and pulled a yellow tablet towards him on the scarred table. "These are all names, Arlen. You were right, they are Russian. I will write them down so you can read them. There is nothing else on the page. As for the mark, it reminds me of a family totem or a business mark that I've seen before in the old Soviet Union. I guess in this country we would call it a logo. But I don't recognize it. I can do some research for you, if you want me to, and let you know what I come up with." He tore the page off the yellow tablet and handed it and the paper back to Arlen.

"Thanks, Alec, I would appreciate it if you could check out that logo. It's good to see you again and it's nice to be back in the old stomping grounds, if even for a short time."

"Well, you're looking good, Arlen. You take care of yourself and stay out of trouble."

"You are a good liar, Alec, but I will try." He got up, turned and grabbed his walker and threaded his way back out of the reporter's room.

By the time he got home, he was exhausted and sick. He lay down without eating lunch and immediately fell asleep for four hours. Then, feeling a lot better, he reached into his pocket for the papers he had folded up at the newspaper office. There were only four names which were followed by the funny symbol out of the ten names on the page. Somehow he would have to see if those names were associated with Meadowview, or whether he would have to try and track them down somewhere else.

That was another quandary. If he went to Mia to get help on the names, she might take the whole thing out of his hands, and he wasn't ready to have that happen just yet. But if he didn't, he couldn't think of any other way to get a list of past residents. He sure wasn't going back down to that record room! For not the first time he wished he had a computer with Internet access. If he did he might have been able even to Google it and get a list.

He was still worrying it around in his mind when there was a soft rap on his door.

"Come in, it isn't locked." He sat up and swung his feet over the edge of the bed. Mia walked in, followed by two gentlemen in dark blue banker's suits.

"Hi, Arlen, I'd like you to meet Mr. Sanderson and Mr. Krevitz from the main office of Meadowview Corporation."

The taller of the two smiled at him and said, "Don't get up, Mr. Arlen, be comfortable."

Arlen decided that he might like this guy. He sure wasn't a replacement for Devon.

"Miss Carson and your nephew finally got through to us about Mr. Devon and his extortion racket. For a long time we didn't understand what she was trying to tell us. But we have been getting calls almost every day from someone I believe is your nephew, George Arlen. He has caused our lethargic organization to get off our cozy chairs and investigate, and we find the whole thing particularly despicable." Arlen was surprised. He had figured that they were still going to try and take his property, only more politely.

The short, stocky man said, "We were sent here to investigate and to set things right for those who have suffered losses and who have been frightened by this person." Arlen chuckled to himself and thought, *they even talk like bankers.*

"I hadn't really been harmed yet, but if he hadn't gotten himself killed I probably would have had to decide if I was going to stay here and give him my property, or to fight him and leave. Or maybe get a couple of broken kneecaps. You guys have a pretty nice place here, and I wasn't ready to give it up yet. But you mean to tell me that you really didn't know about this guy?"

"Thank you for your kind words, Mr. Arlen. No, we didn't, in spite of Miss Carson's attempts to tell us. But we are a big bureaucratic organization, and so, even with Mr. Arlen's calls, we didn't actually figure it out until Mr. Devon was murdered and the police started their investigation. Would you mind telling us just how he approached you and what he said?"

Arlen spent the next several minutes describing his experiences with Devon and then said, "I'm still surprised you knew absolutely nothing about this guy. He obviously wasn't in it alone, because he had all the proper credentials for the job, and he sure fooled the folks here."

"We understand that, Mr. Arlen, but as I said, we are quite a large corporation so things that happen in only one location can be missed for a while. We have spent years and millions of dollars establishing our reputation as a first class reputable service provider, and we don't intend for this situation to destroy what we have built. We have an extensive internal investigation ongoing, and the information you have given us will help a lot."

When they finally left, he collapsed back on his bed, exhausted again. But he couldn't relax. He was really baffled. If Devon wasn't part of the company organization, but had still gotten himself executed, what was that all about? Mrs. Toskini was murdered. Before her murder, Hector Bozeman was killed, and afterwards, Devon. There had to be a tie-in somewhere. He might be able to figure Mrs. Toskini's death and maybe Bozeman's as part of the same scheme, but if Devon wasn't involved in that, then why, oh why was he executed? It made his head hurt, so he tried to close his mind and just relax. As he turned over he thought he heard a faint scraping coming from Pender's room. "Here we go again," he said to himself and pulled himself up to the side of the bed. He grabbed his walker and headed for the door. As he shuffled down the hall, he saw that Pender's door was wide open. He still had more curiosity than good sense, so he pushed his way into the room. He saw Pender picking clothes out of the piles on the floor and stuffing them into a small tote bag.

"Hello, Pender, Stan Toskini is looking for you." He shuffled closer, and then Pender whirled around and threw the bag at his feet. The walker shot across the floor and Arlen fell heavily on a pile of clothes. Pender grabbed him and, without effort, threw him on the bed. As Arlen turned and looked up, Pender was tearing a sheet into strips.

"Well, I guess Toskini was wrong. You really aren't a nice guy."

"I'm not bad man. But you need realize it is my life I am fighting for. You know about notebook. You maybe know I not be here legally. If I let you stop me they will send me home and I die."

"Where you from, Max?" He tried to smile as Pender wrapped the strips of white sheet around his ankles.

"Tajikistan. I was Soviet citizen, but after the collapse of Russia, things was terrible. They put me in jail and I would have to pay to get out. My Anna, she is still there."

"Hey, go easy on that leg. It hurts like blazes." He squirmed but couldn't move from the other's grip.

"I'm sorry. I won't tie you too tight. I just have to get away from here without being caught. Please cooperate."

"Not much else I can do. But why don't *you* cooperate and go see Stan Toskini again. He may be able to help you."

"No! He doesn't know those guys. They would kill him too. I can't let happen. I must go away. You quit looking or they kill you, too. I leave door open so someone find you soon."

With that he grabbed his bag and ran out the door, leaving it wide open. Arlen was in severe pain, but he was more upset by his mixed feelings. He knew someone would find him soon, but he hurt like anything, and he felt really stupid to let himself walk into a situation again.

He finally fell asleep, exhausted. The next thing he knew, he was being gently shaken, and he opened his eyes to see Mia's anxious face bent over his.

"Arlen, Arlen, are you okay? What happened?"

"Boy am I glad to see you. Pender was here. He tied me up. He was packing some things to leave. I couldn't talk him out of it. He is one scared dude. But I don't think he is a real bad guy. He left the door open so I would be found fast. I tried to get him to go back to Toskini's, but he wouldn't do it."

"You mean he has been at Mr. Toskini's and you didn't tell me?" Her relieved look turned to an icy glare.

"Oops, I didn't intend to tell you now." He grimaced as she pulled the sheet strips from around his hands. "Toskini made me promise I wouldn't tell anyone he was there. Stan thought he could help him straighten out his INS mess."

"Well thanks a lot for trusting me! I'm going to stop saving your life."

"I'm real sorry, but he was so insistent. I didn't know what to do. Pender was quite sure you would send him back to be killed if you found out he had phony papers.

"He's right on that score. Sometimes there is nothing we can do but to pick them up and send them back. I hate that part of my job."

"Gosh, does that mean you are human after all?" he snickered. "Ouch, watch it!" She had jerked on one of the strips hanging around his ankles, causing a wave of pain to climb up his spine. "Okay, okay," he laughed, "I'm sorry. You are human even if you do work for the government!"

CHAPTER 24

A fter Mia had helped him back to his room, he phoned
Stan and asked him to have his guys keep on the lookout
for Pender. He wasn't sure where he could go, or how much
money he had to go anywhere. If what he said was true, the
phony ID guys had taken all of his savings. *But*, he thought,
*because necessity was the mother of something or other, and
because Pender was pretty desperate, he might try to run.*
He asked Stan to have them keep an eye on the bus depots
and airport for a while anyway. In spite of what Pender had
just done to him, he really would like to help the guy. He
shouldn't have to be that scared.

The rest of the day Arlen spent in recovering from the
beating his system had taken, but he was surprised that he
was in better shape than he expected to be. His new medication seemed to be doing a good job. So in the middle of the
afternoon he found himself quite hungry. *Sleeping through
lunch will do that for you*, he decided. Then he remembered
that they always had what they called 'threesies' down in the
dining room. It wasn't like the teas at four that he had seen
in England, but they had coffee and sodas and some cookies
or a light cake. He had never gone to one because his appetite hadn't been that great, but now he guessed it was time to
try it out and see what they had. There were several from his

floor waiting at the elevator and he saw Betsy at the edge of the group smiling and waving.

"Oh, Arlen, are you going down to threesies? You usually don't."

"Well, I missed lunch, so I'm a little hungry. I can't afford to lose any more weight." He walked into the crowded elevator behind her.

She turned and said, "You should tell your doctor about that. He could recommend some high protein things for you."

Arlen smiled but didn't reply.

As they waited in the coffee line, Betsy said, "I'll get a table, Arlen."

He was in the decaf line, which was longer than her regular line, so by the time he had gotten his coffee, she had picked a table in one corner of the room, set a couple of plates with scones on the table by his chair, and was waiting for him. As he approached the table she did her little chair trick, pulling the chair out and grabbing his walker, then holding the chair for him so he could abandon his walker and plunk down on the hard seat.

As Betsy folded his walker, she said, "I heard you were hurt again this morning, Arlen, dear, what happened?" She leaned the walker against the table and scooted her chair closer to him.

"Oh, I just put my nose where it didn't belong again," he said.

"I heard that nasty Mr. Pender tied you up." She frowned and touched his arm.

Arlen thought, *boy, gossip races around here faster than the flu.*

"I just heard someone rustling around in his room and when I went in, he was there. He tied me up so that he could get away. He just took a few of his things with him. You know, Betsy, I don't think he is a real bad guy, he's just real scared."

"Where do you suppose he was going?"

"To hide, I would guess. He doesn't intend to get caught again. He may be far away by now."

"I really don't know what's going on with him or what happened with Mr. Devon. It really scares me to be here. I wish I knew what was going on." He felt Betsy's hand shake on his arm.

"I do too, Betsy, I do too."

"Do you think he will go back to Mr. Toskini's?"

He didn't answer and he pulled her hand away as several others from their floor pulled up chairs and sat down. The discussion quickly turned to food. It seems that some of the people constantly complained about the meals.

"I wonder what kind of garbage they are going to serve us tonight," a man growled.

"I don't know. They never serve anything good," another answered.

One of the ladies piped up, "yes, they never have any of the kind of food I like. Look at me, the stuff they serve is making me gain a lot of weight."

Arlen smiled behind his hand, winked at Betty and said, "What kind of food do you want them to serve."

The man frowned at him. "Good stuff."

"It must be pretty good, your lady is gaining weight on it."

The lady frowned at him and said, "well, I never..."

"You're a man, you know what we like to eat. Corn dogs and hot dogs and hamburgers. We haven't had a hamburger here since I first got here."

Betty's soft voice chimed in. "But, sir, didn't you go to the barbecue last night? They had both hamburgers and hot-dogs." She smiled at Arlen.

Short-term memory was sometimes a problem here.

Now, after two scones with jam and two cups of coffee, it was just turning four PM, and Arlen was wondering if he would be able to eat any dinner. But he had noticed again, with his new meds, and with regular meals, his appetite was picking up. Being underweight might not be a problem for long.

Back in his room, he was resting from his exertion and thinking about Pender and Devon and all the others involved in the mess. He decided he was finally getting most of the story pretty well pieced together, but he still couldn't quite see where Devon fit in. If he wasn't part of the gang that had killed Mrs. Toskini, and he wasn't part of Meadowview, who was he? And who was chasing Pender? It could either be the ones who killed Devon or the ones who had killed Mrs. Toskini. Whoever it was, they had Pender really scared. If only he would stop running for a while maybe someone could help him, or at least get a little more information out of him.

The next morning as Arlen was pushing his walker down to the elevators for breakfast, one of his neighbors tapped him on the shoulder and said, "Have you heard? Mia has disappeared. She worked the front desk last evening but didn't come down this morning."

Arlen answered, "Did anyone check her room?"

"Yeah, the nurse supervisor went up this morning. Mia's bed hadn't been slept in. But nothing seemed to be missing. Her TV and her laptop were still there."

Arlen turned and rushed back to his room and called Lt. Crowder, only to find out that he was already on his way. He shuddered as he thought about Mia's predecessor, Hector Bozeman. Arlen had really begun to like Mia, even after their bad start. He hadn't even known that she actually lived at Meadowview.

When the lieutenant came, he knocked on Arlen's door and said, "come on up with me while I search her room."

Arlen answered, "Are you afraid that she might have left some clues to her real role?"

"I don't know, but we have to protect her if we can. Let's take a look."

But they found that her room was neat and not graced with anything that could tell anyone she wasn't exactly what she claimed to be, the supervisor of an assisted care facility.

She had obviously been very careful of her identity, so they ended up with nothing.

CHAPTER 25

"What makes you think I work for this INS, whatever that is? I don't even know what it means!" Mia lay on an old overstuffed couch with her hands and feet bound with duct tape. Two beefy men were standing over her in a dingy basement room. The only light came from a single yellow bulb that was suspended from the ceiling, and the place smelled of dirt and damp.

"Look, we know that your predecessor, Hector Bozeman, was INS. When he died, we knew they would replace him with someone else. That someone was you. Why deny it? You certainly aren't Mia Carson. Your guys didn't do a very good job of giving you a new identity. Now you need to cooperate or you will wind up in the same lake where we put Bozeman."

"It's pretty obvious you have your story all made up. The truth is that I applied for the job when Bozeman died and got it." Mia said. "I don't care what your records say." The shorter of the two men reached out and slapped her hard on the face.

"Have it your own way, lady." We have to leave for a while, but you aren't going anywhere, and when we get back you had better have changed your mind and tell us what you've been up to. Or else!"

The two men turned and walked out of the room. The bigger man reached back and turned out the light. "Have to save energy, you know!" He gave her a crooked grin and left, closing and locking the door.

Duct tape was supposed to be great for everything but wrapping ducts, and it did a good job on her hands and feet. Mia didn't know what she could do, even if she got free. She looked around as she tried to wipe the blood from the side of her mouth. She was in a small room, with only two one-by-two basement windows, placed high on one wall. It was still daylight out, but the light was rapidly fading. There was nothing in the room but the couch she was on and a couple of broken chairs leaning against the cement wall. They were covered with dust and cobwebs. It was obvious that no one spent much time there. She had no idea where she was or even if she was in the same town.

As Mia lay there, she relaxed and started thinking about how she had managed to get herself in this predicament. From childhood she had always wanted to be a police officer. Her father and her big brother were both on the Washington D. C. Police force, and she had her heart set on serving with them.

"Pop, what could be more exciting than to serve in the capitol of our country? You have all the local duties and get to protect all of the Senators and visiting dignitaries. What could be more exciting?"

"D.C. police are some of the best in the country, but there are a lot of other places where they have exciting work, too. Don't limit your options to us. You could be in Homeland Security, or the Secret Service, or in one of the big cities out west."

"Yeah, but you guys have the best job, with all of the foreign dignitaries and important people you get to see."

"Look, honey, don't make your decision based on some kind of a romantic dream. We have our problems and there are lots of negatives in this kind of policing. After a while it all gets to be pretty routine. All I'm saying is that we aren't the only game in town. We would be glad to have you on the force, but look around first."

So, as she was in her junior year at Georgetown University, she took her father's advice and began to look around. At about the same time some federal government recruiters came to the campus, and she later told her father, "I didn't even know the INS had real officers. They do some pretty cool things. I thought they were just border guards or something, but they have a whole police force. I think I'm going to try to get into their investigative unit."

"I figured you'd see something that struck your fancy. I'm glad. It's far better to go into something you are charged up about, than just to go into something because your father did. Go for it."

So she had talked to the recruiters and they were impressed with her resume and it was a done deal. She did well on their tests, and so when she had graduated, she went right into the INS academy and hadn't looked back. And now here she was in this dank basement.

Her mother had cried when Mia told her that she was working as an INS agent. She had never told her mother that she was doing undercover work, which was even more dangerous. She thought, *maybe I should have listened to her. She had only wanted to have one member of her family that she didn't have to worry about every day.*

She tried for an hour to get her hands out of the duct tape, but only managed to make her wrists raw and sore and her mouth bleed more.

As she lay back on the filthy couch, she heard the rasp of the bolt being pulled back on the door. A shiver of fright shook her as the door swung open. An ugly, hawk-faced man stuck his head in the opening and whispered, "Be ready, I'll get you out as soon as I can. It may be pretty tricky, though," with that he pulled his head back and closed the door, banging the lock back in place.

She lay back and rested as well as she could with her hands and legs taped. It seemed like hours before the rattle of the bolt told her that someone was again at the door. She suddenly realized that the room was pretty soundproof. The steel fire door muffled any sounds from the inside and the high windows seemed to point to a backyard. This time when the door opened one of the big men walked into the room. He glanced at her and then sat down beside her on the couch.

"Now look, miss, this isn't something I enjoy, but if you will only realize that I have no choice. I have to take you some place tonight where they will make me do away with you if you don't cooperate. Please don't make me have to do that."

"They are blackmailing you, aren't they?" she answered.

"How did you know that?"

"That's their plan, isn't it? They get you out of your country on phony papers and then blackmail you into helping them, or they will turn you in. Let me go and I will try to help you."

The big man paused for a long minute. "No, miss, I just can't take that chance. You don't know how big this organization is. They would find me and send me back or else kill me, and I just can't let them do that."

"How is Meadowview tied in with them?' Mia tried to sound casual.

"I don't know, miss, they just told me to go over and get you. They don't tell us their plans. Now please think about it. I will be back for you at midnight, and then please tell me you'll cooperate." He stood slowly as if he carried a great weight.

"Thank you for being honest with me. I will think about it and will tell you my decision when you come back. In the meantime, you think about this. If you cooperate with me we may be able to stop these guys and free many people like you that are imprisoned by this gang."

The big man slowly walked out of the room, but at the door he whispered, "Yeah, but you would still have to send us all back," and he quietly closed the door and rattled the bolt shut.

CHAPTER 26

S he couldn't tell what time it was, but she figured it was getting close to midnight, because it had been dark for quite a while. She had just about given up hope when she heard the bolt snap back and the hawk-faced man rushed into the room, his small figure outlined in the light from the hallway.

"Hurry," he whispered, "they are just about to come and get you. I have to get you out of here!" He fell to his knees and started slashing the tape around her ankles with a box cutter. Then he jerked her to her feet. She swayed and sat back down. He grabbed her wrists and frantically cut the tape, slicing her hand in his hurry.

"Go out the door, turn left, you will see some steps. Take them to the top and go out the door and you will be in the backyard. There is a gate to the alley and I have left it unlocked. Hurry! Hurry!" He pulled her to her feet and shoved her toward the door.

"But why...?" She whispered.

"No time, hurry!" He shoved her out the door, and she turned and ran up the steps. As she opened the outside door, she turned and saw the two big men running up the stairs. The hawk-faced man was standing at the top watching them. He screamed "HURRY!" and turned and dived down and rammed his head into the stomach of the first man, causing him to fall into the man behind him. As she slammed the door, she saw that all three men were lying in a heap on the floor. She raced across the yard and out the gate and down the dark alley until she came to a lighted street.

She was still very weak from whatever they had knocked her out with. She staggered down the sidewalk, trying to figure out how to get back to Meadowview or to a police station. She glanced back over her shoulder and saw one of the men pop out onto the street. He was not looking toward her, but as she started to run in the other direction he spotted her, and she could hear the pounding of his feet on the pavement of the quiet street. She reached a corner and turned down a brightly lighted street. Seeing a small café that was still open, she ducked into the entrance and looked frantically around.

A middle-aged woman in an apron came out of the kitchen and said, "What's wrong, dearie? You in trouble?"

"Yes, a man is chasing me. Can you hide me?"

"Hurry, come back into the kitchen. I've got a place back there."

They had no more than reached the kitchen when they heard the door slam open. The waitress motioned to a huge cupboard that was lying on its side on the floor. She picked up the lid and Mia jumped in and lay down and the cover slammed over her.

The cook threw some pots and pans on the lid and turned and walked back into the restaurant area and said, "May I help you, sir?"

"Did a lady run in here?"

"No, I ain't had any customers for an hour. What can I get you?"

"Nothing. Get out of my way," He pushed her aside and ran out into the kitchen. "Is there any other way out of this building?"

"No, and I'll thank you to get out of my kitchen. I don't allow customers back here."

The man looked around, shrugged his shoulders and walked back out into the restaurant and out the door.

The cook whispered, "Stay in there for a while. He may be outside watching. I'll keep an eye out for him. He was a nasty one. How'd you get mixed up with him?"

Mia didn't answer, so the cook said, "you okay, dearie? Can you breathe in there?"

Mia's voice drifted softly out of the box. "I'm fine. I'm just pretty exhausted. Could you call the police and ask for Lt. Crowder? If you can't get him, talk to anyone. Just have them come down here as soon as possible."

"I will do that, but I think I'll wait a few minutes. That clown just walked back by here, and he stopped and stared into the window for quite a while."

"You'd better go out and do something so he won't think you're hiding back here."

"Quiet. He's coming back in." She walked back into the restaurant.

"Change your mind? I got some pretty fresh coffee if you want a cup."

"No, I don't want anything. I told you that. How do you get to the rooms upstairs in this place?"

"That door around the side of the building goes up. You won't find anything up there, it's just a couple of apartments and those folks have probably been asleep for quite a while."

The man walked back to the kitchen door and stared into it and then whirled around and hurried out of the restaurant.

The cook walked back into the kitchen and whispered, "He went upstairs. I think he is pretty suspicious. I better call the cops now." She pulled a cellphone out of her apron and dialed 911. The dispatcher said that she would get in contact with Lt. Crowder, but in the meantime she would send out a couple of patrol cars to keep everyone safe.

Five minutes later Lt. Crowder threw open the restaurant door and rushed in. "Where is she?"

"Where is who, mister?"

"Look, I'm Lt. Crowder, I'm looking for Mia Carson. Where is she?"

The cook laughed. "I got her all boxed up. Come on back." She waved toward the kitchen door.

Lt. Crowder ran back to the kitchen and looked around. "Where is she?"

The cook walked over, removed the pots and pans and pulled open the lid of the big cabinet. Mia sat up and then smiled up at her. "I fell asleep."

Lt. Crowder bent over the box and held out his hand. Mia grabbed it and he pulled her to her feet. "What happened? Who was chasing you?"

Mia smiled wearily and said, "Would it be all right if we talked tomorrow? And would it be possible for you to put an officer in our lobby for the rest of the night? That guy is probably watching what's going on here. He knocked me out in our elevator once. I'd rather he didn't do it again. But I can show you where they were before we go back to Meadowview."

By the time Lt. Crowder, Mia and the police got the house it was empty. They went down into the basement and found that the steel door was closed and locked. It took an hour to force the door open, and when they swung it back they found the hawk-faced man lying on his back on the couch. His neck had been broken.

"That man saved my life!" Mia cried, "Who was he?"

"I don't know, but Toskini told me that Pender said that a hawk-faced man had let him go when they captured him. I think he was on our side, wherever he came from."

Lt. Crowder gently searched the man's pockets. His wallet contained a driver's license, an alien registration card and a library card. He only had two ones in the bill compartment. Mia asked for the alien card and read and reread the name, Alex Bosonovich. She knew that she had to find out more about this man.

CHAPTER 27

The bright morning sun beaming into his room had wakened Arlen early, but he didn't feel like getting up, so he lay there thinking about all that had happened. He was very relieved that Mia was back safe. He was really frustrated at not being able to be a part of everything that was going on. Now another person was dead, and they didn't even know who he was. That made four. Hector Bozeman, Mrs. Toskini, Devon and now this Alex what's-his-name. It all seemed pretty grim for his first venture into assisted living. Maybe they should call it assisted dying! He could visualize being number five and the idea didn't appeal to him even a little and scared him a lot. He was really hoping that things would calm down one of these days. Mia thought she was on to something big, but somehow, those guys, whoever they were, seemed to always be one step ahead. How they knew Mia was INS he couldn't say. He certainly hadn't told anyone. Maybe they just guessed, but it seemed more likely that they had a mole somewhere. Arlen still didn't know too many of the Meadowview guests, so it could easily be someone he hadn't even met.

He didn't know how he was going to do it, but he was going to have to get more acquainted with the inmates, especially the younger ones. Maybe, if one of those guys was in on it, he would let something slip, and he could learn a little.

Or perhaps it was a woman, but he doubted it. It seemed more like a man's job to him. He admitted to himself that he was still a little chauvinistic in spite of his liberal education. Suddenly the idea occurred to him that Mia probably had a list of residents with their birth dates on that fancy computer of hers down in the lobby. He pulled himself up, painfully dressed and got ready to go down and see her.

She was sitting behind the self-same computer he had been thinking about, looking lovely in spite of the bluish-red bruises around her mouth. He noticed her wrists were bandaged and there were broad purplish welts on both of her arms.

"Hi, Mia, have you recovered?" He kept his voice light and casual.

"I'm okay. I was just coming up to talk to you. I'm going to leave Meadowview since my cover has been blown. I can't endanger the people here. That means you are on your own, so my advice is for you to leave it alone, and let us work on it." She wasn't smiling.

"I'm sorry to hear that, Mia, you are a bright star in this place. I've gotten used to having you around. What will I do without you?"

"Oh, come on, Arlen, you don't need me, especially if you quit snooping around. We know someone here is working for them, so just remember you won't have me to let you out of the record room, or to untie you next time. So please be careful and drop the whole thing." She was smiling at him now and the smile seemed to light up her whole face.

"You know I can't do that. My genes won't let me. But I sure will be more careful. I don't have anyone besides you to rely on, except maybe Betsy."

"Well, you be careful, I have grown quite fond of you, and I don't want to see you with your neck broken. As for your needs here, the nurse supervisor will fill in until they can hire another administrator."

"At least tell me what you know about what's going on, and I will see what I can figure out. I need something for my brain to work on or it will atrophy."

"Wait for a little while and I will come up to your room. I don't want to talk too much here, you never know who is listening."

"When you come, could you bring me a list of the guests that are younger than the norm here? I have an idea."

Later, in his room, it became pretty obvious that neither of them knew anything new. Mia had brought a list of younger guests. There were only about five of them, and most had come fairly recently. According to her records, the younger ones didn't tend to stay very long.

Arlen met Nurse Supervisor Wong the next day. She was a small Oriental lady who wore a starched white uniform, which contrasted sharply with her short, straight, jet-black hair. He supposed she had no idea of the turmoil in Meadowview. She was very efficient, *too efficient*, he thought. She never seemed to have time to just stop and talk. He granted that she was doing two jobs, and was a little pressed, but he hoped that she would learn to smile a little more.

About a week later, as Arlen was lying on his bed reading a booklet Stan Toskini had given him, he got a call from Mia.

"Hi, Arlen, I just thought I would tell you that the man who saved my life, Alex Bosonovich, had phony papers. He was what people like to call an undocumented immigrant. The papers were very, very good, but our computers have absolutely no record of him."

"So, what you going to do?"

"We're trying to track him down, but as long as an alien hasn't been in trouble somewhere we have to start from scratch. It's really difficult."

"Thanks for updating me," Arlen laughed and continued, "Too bad you can't thank him."

"Perhaps I will meet him in a better place. Keep yourself safe."

He had no more than put his phone down when Lt. Crowder called him.

"Hey, Arlen, did I wake you up?"

"Nah, I was just talking to Mia. They have no idea who her rescuer really is. He had phony papers."

"Well, I imagine she's glad he was there, anyway."

"That's for sure. You got any new information?"

"Not much. We searched her rescuer's apartment. Found a few things there, but not too much."

"Well? Spill it, what did you find?"

"I'm sorry, Arlen, that investigation wasn't mine, and so I can't really tell you right now. I'll let you know if anything important turns up."

"Thanks a lot."

"Hey, I called you, didn't I? You should be grateful for small favors. Gotta go, bye."

Guess he thinks I'm not reliable, he thought. He was going to have to get the good lieutenant over and feed him a little soft soap. He really needed some new leads.

He lay back down on the bed and began to reflect on a long conversation he had with Stan Toskini the day before.

"You know your trouble, Stan? You don't seem able to separate religion from everyday life. I've never talked to anyone like you before. You seem to think everything has something to do with God."

Stan laughed, "And your point is?"

"Well, I've never been around any of you so called fundamentalists before. It is interesting, in a creepy sort of way. It seems to me sorta like believing in Santa Claus. Most adults don't do that."

Stan roared with laughter. "Hey, I like Santa Claus, too. I even like Saint Nicolas, who is his origin. But God is not a

Santa Claus. My God is the one who made heaven and earth and all of us poor souls."

"Well, if he did, he made a lousy job of it. Is there anyone left who really believes that there was a method and organization in how we all were made?"

"I can't take the time to explain it all today, but there are some books by some pretty credible scientists who can answer some of your questions. I'll bring a couple when I come over."

Are you talking about those crazy folks called creationists? My friends have told me how nutty they are."

"Have you ever met one, or read anything by one?"

"Well, no. Most of my friends are sane."

"Read the books and we'll talk again. You will be surprised. I'm going to improve your mind in spite of your ultraliberal friends."

He suddenly sat up, chuckling at how his mind tended to wander whenever he relaxed, something he almost never did when he was in his prime, working on a story. Besides, when his mind wandered too much it always ended up tossing up the bad things he had done and the mistakes he had made and that always depressed him. He had to get his mind back on the mystery and forget about himself.

The two Meadowview executives knocked on his door right after Arlen had returned from lunch.

"We just thought we would fill you in on what we know, since you were so helpful to us the last time we were here," the younger man said, after Arlen had gotten them settled in his only two chairs. "Actually we don't know a whole lot more than we did then, but with the help of the FBI, we've managed to learn a little more of who Mr. Devon was. He was a member of an international gang out of Baltimore. They seem to specialize in infiltrating large organizations like ours, but we don't know much more than that. The FBI hasn't found the local office of the group."

The other man spoke up. "It is a mystery to us how he got into the Meadowview organization. He just suddenly appeared at a time when things were fluid at this location and from then on everyone thought that someone else had hired him."

The first man broke in, "You can be sure that people like us will be visiting these branches more often to make sure they are running properly. That will include talking more to the guests. They, like you, can tell us a lot."

"The money that came in from the land he extorted never was put into the Meadowview system, of course. It just disappeared and apparently ended up in Baltimore," the first man added. "As a scam, it seemed almost bullet proof, but for some reason Mr. Devon wasn't, and that's a mystery we aren't prepared to delve into. We don't know if he got crossgrain with his own organization or if the people Miss Carson was after had something to do with it."

"We are in the process of filling your administrative vacancy, but we are trying to be very careful. We have made it abundantly clear that we won't allow any more government agents in the position. We also are making sure we don't get someone from either of the organizations that have been interested in us, so it's going to take a while,"

The older man added, "All we really want is a peaceful, successful operation." Arlen could agree to that! "We have absolutely no plans to kick anyone out of Meadowview! In fact, our executive board is trying to figure out some way to subsidize those who outlive their money. We don't believe our agreement with you ever allowed us to arbitrarily make anyone leave, but we have our attorney staff making sure that is the case."

"What do you know about the younger people that move in and only stay a short time and then move out?" Arlen asked.

"We don't know anything about that," the younger man answered. "The referrals are handled locally, but if there was a room available, we normally would accept a guest, no matter what their age. We can't really discriminate on the basis of age."

Arlen smiled at them and said, "I have one last question. Have you satisfied my nephew George that you aren't about to steal my property and kick me out?"

Both men laughed. "Yes, we have talked to Mr. Arlen several times. I believe we have satisfied all of his worries. He is a good nephew. He really cares for you."

"Thanks, I appreciate that. He has helped me over some pretty rough spots after my wife died and I got this malady. I'm glad you satisfied him or I expect I would see him standing in my doorway one of these days ready to pack my suitcases."

CHAPTER 28

A rlen stirred groggily and thought, I've either got to get friends who sleep in or change my ways. I'm too old to keep waking up this way. The phone kept up its jangling until he reached out and brought it to his face.

"Arlen here."

"Morning, Arlen, Stan, have you read the morning papers?"

"No, I'm still asleep," he grumped.

"Our friend the lieutenant has been busy. He found the local office that your Mr. Devon operated out of. They raided it last night and have several people in custody. The paper didn't say much more than that. You'd better call him and see if you can get some more out of him. It might help us to know what happened to Grandma."

Arlen yawned. "He hasn't been too communicative, but I'll try. I'd sure like to know if Devon was tied in with the bunch the INS was after. If they were, I don't imagine Mia will be too happy."

He hung up and then put in a call to Lt. Crowder, but, as usual, couldn't get him on the phone. Instead he got a casual promise that they would have him call back when he could.

So Arlen decided to call Mia and see what she knew.

"Hi, Mia, what do you know about Lt. Crowder's raid on Devon's shop."

"What are you talking about? I haven't heard anything! That lieutenant talks about cooperation and he doesn't even bother to tell me about this? He doesn't know if Devon is part of my investigation! I've had about all I can take of him!"

"Hey, hey, don't kill the messenger. I just heard about it from Stan. It's in the morning papers."

"Oh, Arlen, I'm sorry," she chuckled. "I know it's not your fault. I'm just frustrated that I haven't gotten this case farther along, and my superiors are on my back too. I'll check it out and let you know what I find. Forgive me?"

"Sure, I can understand how you feel. I hope you two can get together and that it helps your case."

The lieutenant called him as soon as he had hung up from talking to Mia.

"Hi, Arlen, hear you wanted to talk to me."

"Hi Lieutenant. Did you know that Mia is pretty mad at you?"

"I suppose so, but we have a job to do, and even though this Devon's group may have a foreign background, they don't seem to be tied together. He once was a secret police officer in the old USSR and his whole crew went into this business after the bust up. They've been in business for quite a while now."

"Well, she believes they are all connected, that they are just branches of the same big organization. I'm sure I don't know, but it seems like you could have clued her in that you were making a raid."

"Perhaps you're right, but this crew seems to be involved in smallish but highly sophisticated scams all over the country. The only tie to Mia's group is that they both come out of the old Soviet Union. The funny thing is, if they are telling the truth, they don't have any idea who did Devon in, or why. It really scared them because it was done so slickly. Maybe that's why they were willing to talk to us. Their big headquarters is back east and as we speak, the FBI is going after them. We're just dealing with the local boys."

"You don't suppose they were just conning you?"

"Could be, but they seemed pretty flustered and jumpy. One thing we are going to have Mia's people do is to check these guy's papers. We may find some phonies among them, too. Apparently Devon's were. But I still think that was the only possible connection to the INS case. It was our bust, fair and square."

Arlen hung up and looked at the big rectangular box that Ben had just laid on his bed. The return address showed that it was from Minneapolis. He pulled his little blade out of the drawer and sliced the tape and opened the top of the box. Another box was inside the cardboard box. This box had a picture of a laptop computer on it. On top of that box was a number 10 envelope with his name on it. He opened the envelope and recognized George's neat cursive.

Dear Unc:

I promised to get you a laptop and I almost forgot. So here it is. It is all set up and ready to go. I hope that Meadowview has Wi-Fi so you can get on line right away. I have set up an email account for you, and Beth says that with Skype she can see if you are taking good care of yourself. If you have trouble with it give me a call. Maybe there is someone there who can help you with Skype if you haven't used it before.

"We are still planning to come out to see you next summer. Take good care of yourself. We were very happy to hear that you are gaining some weight and have more energy. That new med must be the real stuff. God bless you. Oh yes, your password is: 1stClassNewsGatherer. Watch the caps.

Love,

George.

Arlen chuckled and shook his head. "I wish I'd had this a few weeks ago," he said out loud. He opened the box and set the computer on his desk and turned it on. A screen popped up with a nice picture, but he couldn't find any place to type in his password. He finally figured it out and his home screen came up and then he was lost. He didn't even know how to turn it off. It certainly wasn't Windows 7.

He stood up and shuffled over to his bed, threw the box on the floor and lay down. Then he picked up the phone and called Stan. When Stan answered Arlen yelled, "Help! I just got a computer and it is smarter than me."

Stan chuckled and said, "It doesn't take long to be obsolete as far as using a computer is concerned. You want some help?"

"I do. But please don't send me one of your computer geniuses, I wouldn't even understand their language. Just hook me up with someone who uses this stuff. Beth tells me I should try Skype, whatever that is. She says she could see me if I do. Do you understand that at all?"

"I have used it, but I don't know how to set it up. I'll send Toby over. He's pretty good at that stuff, but he speaks plain English and not computerese."

That same afternoon Arlen was taking a nap when his door rattled in its frame. "That must be you, Toby, come on in."

"Hi, Mr. Arlen, I hear you've got yourself a new computer."

"Hello, Toby. Yep. My nephew promised to get me one and I got it today. It's over there on the desk if you want to look at it. By the way, how about just calling me Arlen. Mister sounds so formal."

Oh, I don't think I could do that. I have always been taught that I should respect old people...not that you're old, but you know what I mean."

"Yes, I am old. I don't want to make you uncomfortable, so call me whatever you want to."

"Say, that's a nice computer. We can get you a better screen saver than that. I like a slideshow of pictures myself. Rev said you want to learn about Skype. I can set that up for you. If you know someone that has Skype give them a call while I set it up. I see that this place has an open Wi-Fi, so it won't take long.

Arlen dialed George's number and Beth answered. "Hi Uncle Arlen."

"How'd you know it was me? I didn't even say hello yet."

"Your number is in my phone's address book, so it brings up your name when you call. How are you doing? George is at work. Do you want him to call you?"

"No, you'll do fine. I just wanted to thank you guys for my new laptop. I've got a guy here helping me figure out how to use it, and he asked me to get someone to Skype with, whatever that means. Can you do that?"

"Sure. I'd be glad to. I told George that I could keep tabs on you with Skype. You won't have any privacy at all...I hope you know I'm just joking. Go ahead and we can try it."

In a few minutes Toby had it set up and Beth's smiling face was on the screen. Toby got up and said, "You sit here in front of your little camera, and you can talk to her. Do you want me to leave?"

"No. We won't say anything you can't hear. Have a seat."

"Beth, you look great. Can you see me, too?"

"Sure. You look a lot better than the last time I saw you. Your health is improving."

They talked for a few minutes and then quit, and Toby showed Arlen a few of the new wrinkles in the Windows program. Then he left after telling Arlen that he should get on their website, RocksToby.org.

He spent the whole afternoon on line, looking at sites that talked about the so called Russian Mafia and other organizations that came out of the Baltics. He found out that they were still active in Tajikistan, which was bad news for Pender. He got so interested he almost missed dinner.

As he shuffled into the dining room he saw Betsy watching the door. She picked up her napkin and waved it at him. He went over and sat down across from her. The seats on both sides of her were already taken.

"I thought you might be ill. You usually don't miss a meal, even though you don't eat much."

"I got a new toy today and I just couldn't leave it alone."

"What in the world kind of toy would that be, Arlen dear?"

"George sent me a laptop computer. I can look up all sorts of stuff."

"That's nice. I never thought much of computers. They seem so complicated. What were you looking up?"

"Oh, just some stuff about the breakup of the old Russian Empire and the fallout from that. I learned a lot."

"That doesn't sound very interesting to me. I never did like history." She frowned at him. "Are you trying to find something out about what's been going on around here?"

"Well, I guess that's it. I've just always been interested in history." Arlen looked around and didn't say any more. He realized that the two people who had been sitting on either side of Betsy were leaning across the table to hear what he said. "Lots of people order stuff on line, too. I want to find out how that works since I'm not very mobile. They say there are many more companies on line then a few years ago when I had my big computer. Stan's guy is helping me figure it out."

"You mean one of those big motorcycle guys? Are you sure you can trust them? They look pretty mean."

"Nah, they are really nice guys. Stan is one of them, you know."

Later, lying down in his room, he castigated himself for talking so much when there were lots of people around. *Those people next to Betsy sure were soaking it up. Betsy just brings out my desire to show off a little, I guess,* but he promised himself he would watch it in the future and quickly fell asleep.

CHAPTER 29

Toby looked at his Twitter account and saw a short message. "We have Toskini. Come to Sequoia Motel."

He punched the quick dial for Rocks and, when he answered, he said," I got a message that someone has Rev. Did you get one?"

"Yeah, I got it on my email. What did yours say?"

"We have Toskini. Come to Sequoia Motel. What did they say to you?"

"Mine was a little longer. It said I should come at 3:00 pm and come alone. It's almost three already. I'm goin'. I think someone is messing with the Rev."

Toby turned the key and started his motorcycle. "You aren't going alone. I'm going with you. Where can I meet you?"

"No! I gotta go alone. If Rev is in trouble they won't like two of us coming."

"I don't get it. They told me to come too. Why would they tell you to come alone?"

"Well maybe you're right. I think they are trying to confuse us. Meet me down at the corner of 11th and Main. That motel isn't too far from there." Rocks grabbed his helmet off of his coffee table and ran out to the front driveway where his huge Harley sat.

The two men met at the corner and Toby said, "Since they told you to go alone, why don't you go, and I will stay behind you a little ways so that I can back you up without being right in their faces?"

"Sounds good to me. But I've gotta go. It's three now." He throttled up and raced down the street his exhaust echoing off the buildings on either side.

Toby waited until Rocks had ridden about half a block and then slowly followed him. As he steered his bike down the quiet road he thought, *we should have waited and got some of the other guys to go with us. We haven't thought this out very well. Oh well, it's too late now.* He said out loud, "Lord, if Rev is in trouble, let us help him and get him to safety. If we are being foolish, please protect us as we investigate. Thanks for being with us. Amen."

He watched Rocks drive into the motel lot and park his bike. As Rocks walked up to the building, a door opened, and Toby stopped as he saw him enter a room. As he sat there deciding what to do, a car pulled up beside him, and a man pointed a gun out of the back window and said. "Stop your motor. You are coming with us."

Toby looked at the gun that was only a foot from his face and realized he had no chance to escape, so he turned off his engine and kicked the stands down.

"Get in the car." The back door opened and the man waved the gun at him.

"Who are you guys? Why are you pointing that gun at me? I don't even know you."

"Quit talking and get in."

Toby crawled into the back seat of the sedan and it rolled down the street to the motel and turned into the parking lot and stopped. "Get out!" The man waved the pistol at him again.

Toby got out and the two men led him to the same door that Rocks had entered. One of the men tapped on the door and it opened a crack and then was swung wide open. As Toby was pushed into the motel room, he saw Rocks sitting on a chair, with his hands and feet duct taped and with a piece of duct tape over his mouth. He whirled around, but the man with the gun was directly behind him.

They put him in another chair and duct taped his hands, feet and mouth and taped him to the chair and then all of the men left.

The next morning Stan walked out in front of a small group of bikers that were gathered in his storefront church for Sunday morning services.

"Good morning men. Have any of you seen Rocks or Toby?"

The men looked around, as if expecting to find them in the crowd. Then they all began shaking their heads. One man spoke up. "I seen them at breakfast yesterday morning, but they didn't say that they was goin' anywhere in particular."

"Well, I'd appreciate it if, after the service, you rode around and looked for them. They are supposed to be here leading a Bible study, and they didn't show up. You guys know that's not like those two guys. I'm worried about them."

After the service the bikers fanned out through the city and began searching. It wasn't long before they found Toby's bike. It had been impounded in the police lot because it had been found parked almost in the middle of the street. Another biker found Rocks bike, still parked at the Sequoia Motel. The bikers all congregated around the motel and knocked on every door, but didn't find either of them. One neighbor said, "We were just checking in and we saw a man riding a motorcycle drive in and stop. That's his machine there. He went into room 104."

Room 104 was the only room they hadn't looked in, because nobody had answered their rather loud knocking. One of the men rousted out a very nervous day manager, and he brought a key to the room. "I'm not allowed to do this." He whined. "People are supposed to have their privacy." He looked around at the group of rough looking men, shrugged his shoulders, and opened the door.

The room was empty, but there was a roll of duct tape on the bed and fragments of tape around two chairs that were sitting in the middle of the room. One of the bikers punched 911 on his smartphone and soon there were several blue suited officers on scene.

One of the officers, a sergeant, began quizzing the bikers. Then he said, "You guys never want to cooperate with us when we have a problem, but when it's one of yours you run for help. I'm not inclined to do much about this because it's probably just some gang stuff. They'll show up beaten up, and it will all be over. I'll put in a report, but don't expect much from us." He stuck his PDA in his pocket and walked out to his car.

Meanwhile, Stan had headed over to Meadowview and was pounding on Arlen's door. "Don't break it down. I'm old and slow." He had just waked up from a nap and was feeling pretty cranky. He shuffled over to the door and pulled it open.

Stan smiled at him and said, "I didn't mean to make you grouchy, but I need to talk to you. Can I come in?"

"Of course. Don't mind me. What's going on?" He motioned for Stan to come in and have a seat.

"Toby and Rocks are missing. Our guys found their bikes and where they had been taped up in a motel room, but since then they have just disappeared. I have 25 bikers out looking for them, and they can't find a trace. Do you suppose you could get Lt. Crowder involved? I think it might be something to do with the fact that they have been helping us look for grandma's killers."

"Hang on, I'll call him. He's gotten almost human lately. I even have his home phone number. It being Sunday, I'd guess that's where he is." He picked up his phone and dialed a number. After a short wait he said, "hi, lieutenant. It's Arlen. You got a minute?"

"Sure, I always work on Sunday afternoons. What do you need?"

Arlen told him about Rocks and Toby, and that they thought they might have been kidnapped because they were helping look for the bad guys.

"Have you called the police?"

"Yeah, but they weren't much help. When the biker called them to come to where Toby and Rocks had been tied up, the sergeant just brushed them off because they were bikers. Said he wasn't going to do anything about it. I've got the sergeant's name if that will help."

"Okay, give me his name and hang on a few. I'll make some calls and get that lazy sergeant to do what he gets the big bucks to do. I'll call you back in a few."

Stan stayed at Meadowview for dinner and then left. It was almost seven PM when Lt. Crowder called Arlen back. "I've had an APB out all afternoon, and the sergeant, and quite a few other police officers, have been looking for those guys. The motel clerk was really scared. He said that four really big guys rented the room. He saw Rocks come up on his bike, but just figured he was another really big guy, so he stayed out of sight. We'll keep on it, but they must be holed up somewhere. I've got pictures of them out to all our stations. That's the best I can do. Rocks bike wasn't in the parking lot any more."

CHAPTER 30

Toby woke up and looked around the basement room. Light was filtering in from two very small windows that were on the wall, almost at ceiling level. He reached over and shook Rocks. Rocks jumped up and then sat back down on the edge of the bed where he had sprawled out.

Toby said, "It's morning. What we going to do to get out of this dump? Why do you suppose those guys picked us up in the first place?"

"I think it's because we have been snooping around for Rev and Arlen. It must have something to do with those illegals that murdered that poor little old lady. I guess we must be making them nervous. I don't know how we're gonna get out of here. Do you?"

"No. I wonder where we are. It looks like we are in an old house. I expect our guys are out looking for us. Maybe they will find us, I hope. Shh, quiet. Someone's coming. Get beside the door. Quick." He jumped up and ran and flattened himself against the wall. Rocks ran over to the other side of the door and did the same.

The lock squeaked and someone pulled the door open. A voice drifted through the opening. "I don't want to have to shoot you guys, but I will if you don't get away from that wall and go sit on the bed."

Rocks shrugged his shoulders and nodded to Toby, and they both strode over and plunked down on the edge of the bed. One man came into the room with a tray of food. The other man stayed by the door with an automatic pointed at them. The man set the tray on the floor and said, "The boss wants to talk to you this afternoon. He has a deal for you. You biker guys aren't against making a little money, are you? He can make you a good deal." He turned and walked out of the open doorway and the lock clunked against the doorframe.

Rocks got up and picked up the tray and brought it back to the bed. "It may be to our benefit that they think all bikers are dishonest. I'll be interested to see what they offer us. It may be our chance to get out of here. I'm a Christian, but I sort of get the feeling that I would like to punch a couple of these guys in the nose big time."

Toby laughed and reached for one of the sandwiches on the tray.

The late afternoon sun was fading fast in the little window openings when the bolt clunked and the door opened. A man carrying an automatic stood in the opening. "Come on, you guys. The boss is here. Come through the door one at a time and don't try any funny stuff or I will be forced to shoot you."

Rocks got up off the bed and walked slowly to the door. Toby hesitated and looked around for any kind of a weapon he could fine, but the room was bare except for the old bed, so he got up and walked through the opening behind Rocks.

There was another man outside the room, pointing a rather large revolver at them. He motioned for them to walk up the stairs and then stepped in front of them and led the way. As they reached the top of the stairs they saw that they were in the kitchen of the house. The man led them on into what seemed to be the living room, although there was almost no furniture in the room. They saw a man sitting on a small sofa and two straight backed chairs sat facing him. The man with the gun pointed to the chairs and Toby and Rocks sat down facing the couch.

The man looked at them for a couple of minutes and then said, "You guys want to make some money?"

Rocks looked at Toby and then back at the man and said, "We aren't allergic to a little money, as long as we can do it and stay out of jail."

"What I want you to do isn't illegal. I just need your help to get a man's attention. Do you know a man named Jason Arlen?"

"You mean Arlen?"

"Yeah, that's the guy. We need to talk to him, but he refuses to talk to us. We have some business with him and his stupidity is costing us money. He is in a deal with us and he isn't doing his part. If we could talk to him we think we could persuade him that he would make more money if he cooperated. That's all there is to it."

"Look, mister, we won't be part of something real illegal. We don't mind bending the law a little, but if you are going to hurt this guy we don't want any part in it."

"No, no. It is strictly a business conference. We think we have enough information to make him change his mind. We would never hurt him."

Toby pointed to the two men who were standing behind them, still holding the guns. "Your apes don't seem to think this is just a business deal. If that's all it is, tell them to quit pointing those guns at us."

"I'm sorry, I can't do that. You bikers are known to react pretty violently sometimes. I just have them here to keep this meeting peaceful. If you don't cause trouble things will be okay. We just want you to bring him over here so I can talk to him. I think he will listen to you. That's all. I will give each of you one hundred dollars if you can pull it off. That's a pretty fair deal isn't it?"

"Do you know where our bikes are?"

"My guys will get them back for you. But remember. Look at these guys behind you. They will be watching every move you make, so you won't pull anything funny."

"Toby scratched his head and said, "Sounds like a pretty good deal to me. When do we get our C note?"

"You bring him here and the money will be waiting for you, and then you can leave and go about your business. I know you won't bring the cops, because the cops wouldn't believe a bunch of bikers, but play it smart. If you try anything, nobody will be here but the pickup men, and they know how to take care of themselves. Do we have a deal?"

"Sure. I can use a hundred bucks. I'm in." Rocks turned to Toby. "How about you?"

"Yeah. I don't see no problem doing that." He turned to the man and said, "you gonna let us go now?"

"No, we'll keep you here until tomorrow. That way we can get your bikes for you, and you can figure out how you are going to do it." He motioned to the gunmen and said, "Take them back down to the basement, then get them some food."

The gunmen motioned, and Rocks and Toby stood up and followed the men back to their prison. One gunman closed the door and locked it. Toby walked over and plunked down on the bed and said, "What do you..." Rocks waved his arms and put a finger to his lips. Then he put a hand to his ear and pointed in a circle around the room. Toby nodded and said, "What do you think about the deal. Do you think they will really give us one hundred bucks? Sounds like a pretty easy job to me."

Rocks walked over to the bed and sat down beside him. "Yes, it's a sweet deal. Nothing illegal, yet we make some pretty good money. Arlen won't mind coming here with us. We'll get him as soon as they give us our bikes. We really fell into something good."

"I hope they bring us something good to eat. I'm really hungry."

Rocks laughed and said, "There's only one lousy thing about this deal."

"Yeah? What is that?"

"I got to sleep in the same bed with you tonight. You forgot to shower this morning."

"You don't smell so sweet yourself."

The door opened and a man entered, carrying a tray. "Here's your dinner. I brought some really big hamburgers. You guys are pretty big. You must eat a lot. I'm glad you are going to cooperate. I'd hate to have to shoot you."

"Thanks a lot, pal. I wouldn't mind shooting you. You get on my nerves. Go away."

"Don't get wise. I could take this food away if you want to play games."

Rocks waved his hand. "Nah, don't get riled, my friend just has a big mouth. Thanks for the food."

After the man had left Rocks winked at Toby and then said, "You big dummy. You want these guys to starve us to death? Why don't you keep your big mouth shut?"

"Look, man, you ain't my boss. So bug off. I'll say what I want to say. I'm not too happy being in this deal with a dummy like you. I hope you don't screw it up. I want my C note." He lay his hand on the bed and wiggled his thumb back and forth.

Rocks saw it, smiled a little and said, "Oh well, I guess we'll get our money from these bozos. Let's eat." He picked the tray off the floor and set it on the bed.

CHAPTER 31

T he next morning passed slowly for Rocks and Toby. Nobody brought them any food and they heard no footsteps upstairs. Finally, about one in the afternoon, Rocks whispered, "Listen. I hear my bike. I think I hear yours too. Do you think they will really let us out?"

"I guess we'll soon find out."

The lock on the basement door scrunched, and a big man holding a gun stepped into the room. "You guys come on upstairs. The boss wants to talk to you again." He waved the gun towards the door.

Rocks and Toby stood up and walked out through the opening and up the basement steps. The gunman led them into the living room and pointed to the same two chairs.

The boss was sitting on the small sofa again, and smoking a smelly cigar.

"You guys understand the deal?"

Rocks answered, "Sure. It doesn't sound too complicated, All we have to do is bring Mr. Arlen back here and you hand each of us one hundred smackers and we go away."

"That's right. But if you try to contact anyone else or bring anyone else back you are dead men. Do you understand me?"

"Sure, sure. Look, I need that hundred. I got to pay the insurance on my bike. You don't have to worry about us."

"Just know that you will be watched. You won't have a second that you are out of our sight."

"Okay, okay, just stay out of our faces or we may not be able to get him to come. He's no dummy."

"You don't have to worry about that. Now get out of here and bring him back before the end of the day or you don't get your money."

Rocks and Toby stood up and headed for the front door. The gunman walked ahead of them and opened the door. A gauntleted fist flew through the opening and connected violently with his nose, hurling him back and on the floor. Toby dove down beside him and grabbed the gun and aimed it at the boss, who was running toward the hallway. "If you don't stop I will have to shoot you, mister. I'm a good shot." He fired the gun and a bullet skimmed by the man's head and plunked into the back wall. He screeched to a stop and raised his hands.

At the same time men streamed in the front door and one of them hollered, "Are there any more of them in the house?"

Rocks said, "There was one more guy here. I don't know if there are any more. Be careful. They have guns."

Several of the bikers grabbed the boss and the man on the floor and began binding them with a roll of duct tape. The one who had hollered at them said, "Give me that gun and we will search the house. We got it surrounded."

Toby said, "I'm calling the police. Why don't you wait until they get here?"

"I can handle it. Go ahead and call them. I'll have them all rounded up by the time they get here."

The back door burst open and a man's body was hurled in through the opening. "Hey, guys, we caught this guy trying to get away. He's a lousy shot, but he got Henry in the arm. I called the paramedics."

Rocks scratched his head. "How did you guys ever find us? We didn't even know where we were."

"Man that was pretty simple. We just had someone keep his eye on your bikes. When a couple of guys came around and picked them up we followed them. We had a plan all worked out. Pretty neat, huh?"

Rocks burst out laughing. "How did you know that they were going to get our bikes? They might have just taken us out and shot us. You weren't smart, you were lucky."

"Well, if you feel that way, we'll give you back to these guys and go home."

Toby said, "Don't listen to Rocks, I'm glad you came however you found us. We were supposed to do a dirty on Mr. Arlen, and we couldn't do that. He's a friend of Rev."

Two big blue suited police officers rushed through the door, their guns drawn. "All right, put your hands on your heads and line up against the wall."

Rocks said, "Hey, it's us that called you. Put your guns away, we got it covered."

"We'll see about that. Now do as I said. You bikers always are looking for trouble. Who is this guy that is all trussed up?"

Toby said, "He's the guy who had us kidnapped. I don't know who he is."

"Just a guy from another biker gang no doubt. I sent for a van to take you all down to the station. So shut up and stand still until it gets here."

He turned and looked as another person rushed into the room. "What's going on, sergeant? Why are you holding these men? Put away your guns."

"And who are you to barge in and order me around. These bikers are up to no good. I'm going to take them downtown. So butt out or I will take you with them."

"Sergeant, if you would like to keep your stripes you will ditch that snotty attitude and do as I say. I am Lt. Crowder. I know these men and they have been held captive for two days. It seems they were smart enough to escape without our vaunted help. So, I say it again, put your guns away. And by the way, sergeant, you can report to my office the first thing in the morning. You are a disgrace to your uniform."

The sergeant holstered his gun and stomped out of the room. The other police officer put his weapon away and followed him.

"Sorry about that, guys. Some of our officers have had some pretty rough times with certain bikers, so they paint you all with the same brush. I don't think the sergeant will do it again, if the commission allows him to stay on the force. We'll take care of these guys. Are you two okay? Doesn't look like they roughed you up."

"Nah, the good Lord protected us, and our friends rescued us. What more could we ask for."

CHAPTER 32

S trange as it seemed to Arlen, things suddenly appeared to have come together in his brain. There were still a few loose ends that he had to email about to his pal down at the paper, who was an expert on the old Soviet Union, but now he was sure that he understood what was going on. He knew that Mrs. Toskini had been on to something much bigger than she had realized and gotten her neck broken for her curiosity. Her big mistake was to have put it all down in her address book in plain sight. Even that might not have been so bad, he figured, but she had made the fatal error of confiding in somebody she really trusted. At first he had thought it must have been a relative, or at least one of the many people who had trooped in and out of her room every day. He had finally begun to realize that it couldn't be one of them, but had to be someone who lived at Meadowview. She was a friendly person and pretty naive, he thought. She was a Christian like her grandson and they seemed to trust everyone.

He didn't know exactly when it had come to him, but now he was sure. He knew who it was and why. It had to be a person who listened to him down in the dining room. He just had to curb his bragging mouth. It seemed so obvious to him now. It had been Devon's death that had thrown him off. It still didn't seem to fit the rest of the plan. He wasn't sure why he had been killed, but he was sure it was part and parcel of all that had happened.

So he set up his plan and then spent the week worrying if it would work, or if he would end up dead.

Now, as he sat on his bed, he was just beginning to have serious doubts, to wonder if he wasn't wrong after all, and if he wasn't going to look a little more foolish than usual, the door of his cubicle rattled.

"Arlen, it's me, Betsy. I'm here, let me in." The door continued to rattle.

"It's open, come on in," he shouted at the door.

The door swung open and Betsy walked in, followed by about the biggest man Arlen had ever seen. He wasn't just tall; he was so wide that he had some trouble getting in the doorway. Arlen arched his eyebrows at Betsy, and she nodded toward the hulk and said, "I hope you don't mind, I brought Mike with me. He is an old friend from where I used to work, and he is as interested in this case as I am. I have been telling him about it and I thought he might be able to help us solve it."

"Well, grab a seat. I need your help to solve this case." he motioned to the desk chair and the guest chair. Big Mike prudently took the desk chair and not his thin guest chair.

"Tell us what you have found out, Arlen, dear. You told me you finally had some answers when you called. We'll be glad to help you."

"You always complimented me on my skills as a reporter. I think I did some good this time."

"I know, you were really a good reporter. I often read your columns."

"You couldn't have followed my columns for too long, Betsy, you haven't been in this country that long."

She frowned at him. "Whatever do you mean? I have been in this country for years.

"I'm sure you have papers that say that, just like you have papers that prove that you are a legal immigrant." He noticed that the big man was sitting even straighter in his chair and his fists were clenched.

"It was Devon that fooled me. I didn't know how you two were tied together. Did he work for you or did you both work for the syndicate?"

"Why Arlen, what do you mean? That nasty Mr. Devon really scared me. After all, he took my property too. You surely can't believe I had anything to do with that."

"I don't exactly know how you were related to Devon, but I believe you really did get scared of him. Not because of your so-called property, but because he began working outside of the envelope and you were losing control. His organization was starting to interfere with yours, and so you had him eliminated. He was a smart, tough guy and was finding out too much about your work. So you simply had to get him out of the way. I wouldn't be surprised if your friend here didn't do the job. He looks the type."

He pointed at the big man and continued, "I don't know how you got into this, Betsy, but the whole thing stinks. Maybe this Russian Mafia had something on you, and you had to cooperate, but you had lots of chances to get out of it. I'll say this for you, you are a good actress. I was beginning to really like you. You keep these people in Meadowview after the hoods make them phony papers, and while they are busy extorting all the rest of the money they brought over to live on. When they've got the poor saps' money, you force them to leave. You weren't pikers, you handled people from all over the old SSR's."

He continued, "You took anyone who still wanted to get out of the mess of the fallen Communist system. Of course, they had to have one more thing; they had to have a fair amount of money. Then you had a double grip on them. If you didn't get their money you threatened to turn them over to Immigration, and if that failed you always had Devon or Big Mike to scare it out of them. A sweet deal all around. Did you make a lot of money or did they just have to threaten to expose you too? I suppose this many years after the end of the Soviet Union your bosses are getting hard up for people to rescue. I have to tell you, Betsy, I feel a little sorry for you in spite of myself."

By this time Big Mike was standing up and leaning toward him. Betsy grabbed his arm and pulled him back down in the chair.

"You self-righteous Americans!" she screamed. "You have no idea of what we people have gone through after the collapse of the old Soviet Union and even today. There were no jobs and no food and the old police became gangs preying on us ordinary people. Yes," she growled, "I was just an ordinary person, but I am never going back to that life! I'm sorry you got involved, Arlen," she said in a quieter voice. "I really have come to like you, but you should have just retired and shut up. Your nosy streak has made it impossible for me to let you go. Yes, I had Devon killed. He was from another organization and had his own scam. As long as he didn't interfere with our operation, it didn't matter. But he saw what was going on and wanted a cut of our business, and I had no way to give him that. I am just a little person in this organization. They would just as soon get rid of any of us who caused trouble. What else could I do?"

There was a tremor in her voice now. "They have very efficient ways to eliminate people here, as well as in the old country." The growl was back as she shouted, "We took care of Bozeman and would have gotten Mia if that little weasel of a man hadn't interfered. Now Mike is going to have to arrange an accident for you, and you will go the way of that nosy old Toskini woman. She knew every person we placed in here. I still don't know how she did it, but I hope your precious lieutenant still wants to believe it was an accident. He will also think that about you. He knows you are unstable on your feet, so when you fall and smash your head against the dresser it will be so sad. Mike, go ahead. I'm leaving. I can't stand violence. I saw enough of it in the old country."

As she turned to leave, Mike swayed up out of his chair and reached for Arlen. At the same time the bathroom door flew open and Lt. Crowder charged out, followed by two uniforms. Mike had grabbed Arlen tightly around the waist when Lt. Crowder hollered and pointed a blue-black service revolver at him.

Arlen rasped in Mike's ear, "You aren't stupid, Mike, and I don't think you are suicidal. Those uniforms are carrying great big guns and there's only one way out of here." Arlen gasped for breath, but the words worked like magic. Mike let go, raised his hands and interlocked his fingers behind his neck. He obviously had been through the drill before.

Betsy, on the other hand, went wild. She raced back and climbed right up Lt. Crowder and would have gone clear over the top of his head if he hadn't thrown his arms around her and hugged her in a bear-like grip. Arlen didn't think the man had it in him. He was still trying to clamp down on her hands while she struggled and tore deep scratches down his cheeks. Finally one of the uniforms was able to help him push her down on the chair. Once she was down, her whole body sagged. "Arlen, you will have this on your conscience the rest of your life if they send me back there. I can't go back." She put her face in her hands and began to sob.

"Well, Betsy, or whatever your name is, I don't imagine you have to worry about going back for quite a while. I think the lieutenant has plans for you that involve a good, comfortable American prison. No doubt at least one murder charge will stick and I don't think your organization will spring for a lawyer for you."

She was still crying as the uniforms led her out of the overcrowded room.

EPILOGUE

H aving an overcrowded room seemed to be getting to
be a habit. Today Stan Toskini, Mia, Lt. Crowder and
Max Pender were all trying to find a place to sit. The lieutenant was perched on the edge of the desk and Mia was sitting in his desk chair. Max sat uncomfortably in the guest
chair and Stan sat next to Arlen on the bed. Even George
was there. He had flown out and was sitting on the floor next
to the bed.

"So, Arlen, tell us how you figured this all out," Stan
turned on the bed and faced him. "I sure was stumped. I knew
Max was just a pawn in someone's game, but I never did
figure out who the players were. Max is a good guy and we
are trying to get some relief for him from the INS. Mia here
has been nice enough to give us a big hand." He turned and
waved at her and she smiled in return but didn't say anything.

Max Pender interrupted. "Please, you could stop calling
me Max Pender? I never like that name. My name is Firuz
Sarhad. That is a fine Tajik name."

"Sure, I will be glad to do that. Maybe we can convince
Mia to tell us her real name, too. Anyhow, Pender's situation...
sorry, Sarhad's situation gave me my first clue about Betsy.
You and I knew what he was doing and where he was when
he was at your place. I never told Betsy, but she knew – she
asked me if he was going back to your place, and unless you

213

weren't who you claimed to be, and unless all those motor-cycle guys were lying, she was the only one who could have known and told the syndicate where he was. I didn't even tell Mia." He smiled in her direction. She threw a fake frown at him and then smiled back.

"Besides, she always seemed to be wheedling informa-tion out of me. I was flattered at first, thinking that she was complimenting me on being such a super reporter, and I must admit I was lonely and her closeness was like a tonic to me, but finally I caught on, even though I didn't want to believe it, I caught on.

"I used the listing of the younger inmates, sorry, I mean guests, that Mia gave me, and I found that each of them had papers from the same bureau, signed by the same guy, even though they came from all over the Old Russian Union. Individually they weren't obvious, but when we put them all together they told the story.

"Then Max told Stan about his experience with Mrs. Toskini's address book, and we found a page in Max's room with part of a list in Cyrillic script, and some of them had the same symbol. Sorry about that ...Firuz...I'll get used to your name soon." He waved at the other man who tried to smile back, but instead just managed a worried frown.

"I found all of them all on Mia's list. My friend at the paper found out that the moon symbol is the logo of one of the bigger Russian Mafia type gangs. I don't know how Mrs. Toskini knew that, or if she did."

"So after I had it figured out, all I had to do was the hardest part, which was to get Lt. Crowder here to agree to my little game. He finally caved in and the rest is history, as they say. It wasn't hard to convince Betsy that I had found out something important that I would tell her if she would come to my room. I told her I was afraid to tell her anywhere else. I was scared for a few minutes that she wouldn't bite, but the lieutenant's scratched face shows that she did!" The lieutenant did a little bow from the waist and laughed.

"I'm still not sure I should have let you do it," the lieutenant smiled from his perch on the desk. "That big guy coulda broke you in two pieces before we got off a shot, even allowing that I woulda hit him and not you."

"Well, thank you for going along. Big Mike made me pretty nervous at first, but he seemed to have a strong desire to keep on living, and he was used to a lot nastier police force than you guys."

"What about the little man who saved Max and Mia, who was he?" Stan asked.

"He just seems to have been another one who was trapped by the system, but who finally decided enough was enough. He was a very brave man. He would rather die than let them kill Max or Mia."

"Mia tells me that the FBI and the INS have raided the organization offices in Washington D. C. And she also said that she understood that the Tajik police have found parts of the gang operating right out of downtown Dushanbe and have raided them too. Isn't that right Mia?"

Mia nodded and said, "The State Department has done an investigation of Tajikistan and the mafia type gangs are still there and many Tajik police departments are still pretty prone to taking bribes, so there is a good chance we can get Mr. Sarad into the country as an asylum seeker. I'm working hard on it and on getting his wife here as well. And I'm sorry, Arlen, I can't tell you my real name. I'm still an undercover agent."

"Well, Mia Carson is a nice name, even if you don't exist. Meadowview has instituted some more safeguards in their system of vetting new guests as well as new hires. They really are a legitimate business trying hard to make their places pleasant, livable sites. And they are that, in spite of this occasional overcrowding of some of the rooms."

Arlen laughed and then punched Stan with his elbow and added, "I just found out that you learned about that nice Mrs. Dumont, the missionary lady living here, and have been coercing her into trying to undo my 'liberal media bias!' I ask you, who is the biased one around here?" They all laughed.